THE BOY WHO DIED

B. MOON

For the real boy who did die.

CONTENTS

1

NEW YEAR, NEW ME

MARCIE

I SLING my backpack over my shoulder and step out of my apartment onto the sunny breezeway outside. Early September in Virginia retains most of the heat of summer, so I wipe instant sweat off my forehead before my brown curls can catch in it. This semester is going to be different. That means not showing up looking like a drowned rat, even if I doubt anyone in my photography elective is going to care.

Birds sing as I lock the door then test the knob to make sure it actually locked. A voice in my head that sounds suspiciously like Dana, my therapist, reminds me I'm not supposed to be indulging those instincts. I'm safe here. The only person I've been in danger from since setting foot on the campus of Ardent University is myself, and she's getting out of my way this year. I unlock the door, lock it again, and walk away without testing the knob.

My heavy backpack bounces against my shoulder. I don't want to have to return to my apartment between classes, even if it's technically on campus, and the weight of my books reminds me exactly

1

what kind of day I'm in for. A long one. My very first semester with a full course load. I massage my shoulder and shrug on the second strap to even out the weight. Nursing textbooks aren't light.

But I'm not worried. All summer, I talked with Dana and the guidance office. Both of them asked me a dozen or more times if I was sure a full slate of classes wouldn't lead to what they called "a repeat of last time" and what I call "honestly, a pretty minor mental breakdown, considering." But I am not thinking about that. I'm thinking about the fact that I told them I was sure so many times that they both believed me, and now I have my very first college elective to look forward to. My outlook feels light and bright, and I take a second to categorize the feeling like Dana taught me.

Hope. I smile and stride down the wide, cobblestone path cutting through the main quad toward the art building. This is going to be a good year if it kills me.

Emerson Hall, a glass-covered building that hosts most of the art classes, welcomes me through its wide-open double doors. If I'd lived a different life, most of my classes would've been here. But after months in the institution, I wasn't able to face the idea of grim professors judging my performances like the musclebound nurses judged my finger painting and macaroni necklaces for any sign I was a danger to myself or others. I haven't even entered the building since then. It's light and airy, like I remember from the tour Ryan and I took so many years ago. As always, his name hits me like a spear to the chest. I suck in a deep breath and plunge forward.

The photography class is on the far side of the building from the door in a room covered in windows. A handful of desks sit haphazardly around the room, and a middle-aged woman wearing a blazer with elbow patches looks up from one of them as I walk in.

"I'm Professor Washington," she says. "I love an early student. Really shows the dedication you need to get the shot in the real world. Take a seat, and we'll wait for the rest of the stragglers to wander in."

I nod and surreptitiously check my watch as I claim a desk near the back. Twenty minutes early. Dammit! I tried so hard to arrive a chill, normal five minutes ahead. I'll just do better tomorrow.

Minutes tick away. Professor Washington scribbles in a tiny notebook balanced on her desk. I pull out my laptop, then the simple camera suggested for the course. A few more students filter in. As always, they're all a few years younger than me. Between my reduced course load and the six months I lost to the institution, I'm entering my sixth year attending Ardent. At least I've got kind of a young face. I never lost the baby fat in my cheeks, and I like to keep my hair braided back away from my face in a way my roommate, Heather, says makes me look like an orphan on Ellis Island.

A guy sits in front of me, and my breath catches. His hair is the exact same golden blond as Ryan's in the summer. My rib cage squeezes, crushing all the air out of my lungs. My hands shake. I clutch the edges of my desk to try to still the tremors.

Dana's voice, easy and certain, pours over my thoughts. *Breathe. Three reasons he's not Ryan.*

I inhale. The guy in front of me is shorter than Ryan's 6'3" by a few inches.

I exhale. Ryan lived in goofy graphic T-shirts his mom picked up for him at the local thrift store, and this guy is wearing a kind of ridiculous blazer.

I inhale. The guy in front of me has thick, muscular arms. Despite his height and his few seasons on the basketball team, Ryan hated sports and barely had enough muscle to lift some of his older cameras.

And the most important one? The Dana in my mind taps her pencil against her clipboard.

Ryan is dead. The guy in front of me isn't Ryan because I watched Ryan die, and I remember every second like it was yesterday. I exhale shakily and relax my grip on the desk.

The guy in front of me twists in his seat to reveal a thick, blond mustache. "Can I borrow a pencil?"

I almost laugh as I hand over my spare. What a stupid close call. He looks nothing like Ryan. I fiddle with the settings on my new camera as the last of the desks fill up. The moment class actually starts, Professor Washington stands and begins handing out syllabi. There's no reason to stress today. I doubt I'll be doing anything trickier than reading paragraph five on page two aloud this week. I relax into the flow of class.

"In addition to the two photography expeditions I'm leading on the eighth and the twenty-seventh," the prof says as we approach the end of class, "we have three others, to be led by an actual, working photographer. You're very lucky." She smiles conspiratorially. "Please help me welcome Ben Andrews, the newest photojournalist at the *Ardent Weekly!*"

I clap politely with everybody else, but I'm too busy circling the expeditions Professor Washington will be leading. Her attendance policy is lax as long as people turn in the work, but I'm not going to lose my chance to actually go out in the field with her.

A light, teasing laugh bounces off the windows, and my stomach drops to my toes. He sounds exactly like Ryan. I inhale and look up, ready to start listing differences.

There are none. The man standing at the front of the class, waving his hands to try to get people to stop clapping, looks exactly like my high school best friend, plus the six years I've been without him. His hair is a little longer, curling around his ears instead of shaved tight to his skull. He's grown into his hands and his ears. He wears the sort of preppy, short-sleeved button-down with a tiny pattern we used to make fun of people for. But there's nothing else to separate him from the boy I knew.

"All right, I'm not exactly Ansel Adams." He smiles self-consciously. "I just moved here from a little town in Illinois, and—"

That's Ryan's smile, the one he used when people told him he was so tall he had to play basketball. My stomach lurches. My heartbeat drowns out the rest of his words.

Inhale for three. Hold for three. Exhale for three. Still Ryan. I pinch myself until my jagged nails break the skin. Still Ryan. I shut my eyes, rub them, and open them again. Still Ryan. My rib cage caves in on my lungs as I fight through every goddamn exercise Dana ever taught me, looking for anything that will make this hallucination go away.

It has to be a hallucination. Ryan is dead. He's dead! I saw his blood, still taste it sometimes. But if it's a hallucination… then I'm losing my mind again.

Professor Washington claps her hands, and I jump.

"All right, that's Ben. Why don't the rest of us go around and introduce ourselves? Name, and why you decided to take this class." She smiles. "I decided to teach photography because I think there's nothing more beautiful than giving others the gift of art."

Oh, God, they want me to talk. To talk without throwing up. My skin vibrates as if attempting to escape from my body.

"And you?" Professor Williams looks at me.

So does Ryan. Ben. Ryan. I swallow.

"Marcie Holt," I manage. "Needed an art elective."

Professor Williams purses her lips and turns to the next student. Ben doesn't. He lingers on me. There's something in his eyes I don't recognize. I tear at the skin around my thumbnail.

"That's it for today," Professor Williams finally says. "I look forward to—"

I lurch out of my seat, bolting for the door. It doesn't matter what she thinks of me. I'm changing electives.

2

NO WAY OUT

Marcie

Nothing else in that time slot. I can rework my whole schedule and drop one of the core nursing classes I need to graduate, setting me back another semester, or I can stick with photography. I spend the rest of my day turning the words over and over like there's a loophole I'm just not seeing. The rest of my professors blur. I get lost in the familiar halls of McKinley, the science building. Somehow, I make it back to my apartment. My hands shake as I unlock the door without testing to see if it was locked all day. I'm not supposed to indulge.

I don't want to know.

"Heather?" I call as I step inside.

Silence. I drop my keys on the shoe rack-table combo in the tiny rectangle of space Heather calls our foyer. She must still be at work at the newspaper on campus. I spent the whole summer hearing about what an amazing opportunity being a staff writer for the *Ardent Weekly*—or, as she calls it, the *Arkly*—is for a junior like her. I like her well enough, but sometimes I can really feel the age gap.

Just in case, I peer into the kitchen over the breakfast bar as I pass

—nothing but peeling laminate and dishes I need to wash—and detour through the living room. The massive, squashy orange couch Heather arrived with doesn't even show signs of someone recently sitting down, and it holds onto butt prints for several hours. I am home alone.

I sit on the couch and take a deep breath. I could call Dana. She always says she's open for emergency sessions. But, God, I promised her I had my shit together this time. I don't want to go back to everyone looking at me like I'm the crazy girl.

With a yell, I flop back against the cushions. I can't lose my semester. I can't lose my progress. Maybe I couldn't dispel the hallucination in class, but there's no way Ben looks as much like Ryan as I think.

"Okay," I say out loud, totally not making myself seem even crazier. "I just have to prove that my brain is playing tricks on me. Then, I'll be normal again."

With trembling fingers, I pull out my phone, open it, and plug in the second password that takes me to the folder of pictures of Ryan I haven't gotten rid of. If Dana ever found out about this, she'd be so disappointed, but I can't live a life where I never see him. Ryan's mom didn't approve of social media; she thought he was going to get kidnapped by a pedophile or something, so I only have the pictures I took. I swipe through them one by one. He sits in the branches of our tree, sticking his tongue out at me. His eyes are the same laughing, pale blue I remember. The same color as Ben's.

Stupid. I swipe to the next one. At our lunch table, he grins with his arm slung around Theresa, the final member of our trio, who holds a set of bunny ears behind his head. My throat grows thick, and tears threaten. Last one, then I'll look for pictures of Ben.

A black-and-white picture of him perched on the rock in front of school with his chin on his hand. He made me take the picture and save it for the documentary they'd make about him someday.

I shut my phone as the first tear slips out. I'm indulging, and that's more likely to make me crazy than anything else. I scrub the tear away, sniff back a second one, and pull out my laptop. *What did he say his name was?* Ben Andrews. I type that into the search bar of the first social media I have open and groan. A hundred thousand results within a hundred-mile radius. This is going to take a while.

The living room grows dark around me as I plug his name into social media after social media. Ben Andrews. Benjamin Andrews. B. Andrews. Lots of accounts, but none of them match what he looks like. Nothing, nothing, nothing. In a fit of frustration, I open a regular search engine and type his name with the word "photography" on the end. The page populates with results, and I click on the very first one.

It's a portfolio website. Simple, modern layout. I click on the "about" tab. No picture, but a short description. This Ben Andrews is a freelance photographer for hire in the greater Peoria area. Indiana. The Ben in class said he was from Illinois. It also references Ansel Adams as an inspiration. My stomach turns. This has to be the same person. I click on the "portfolio" tab and pray for a self-portrait so I can convince myself I was just being dramatic.

Dozens of highly saturated rectangles fill the screen. My heartbeat roars in my ears. This is beyond indulgence; this is sickness. I'm stalking my professor! Well, my professor's guest lecturer, but stalking is stalking. I have to stop.

I click on the first picture. A beautiful woman curls around the trunk of a tree, a gauzy, flower-studded robe hiding all the private parts of her while making it very clear that she's naked underneath. Next. A man stares out a window, lit and framed in such a way that I can only see a neon-red sheen on his hair and the edge of his jaw. Next. Another woman. Next.

The pictures start to blur, and a distant part of my brain picks out patterns. Almost all of them feature people. No self-portraits. Not a lot of men at all. Ben obviously prefers female subjects, and suggestively scantily clad ones at that.

Not all of his photos are of women, but those that are show a specific type. There's some variance, but most of his shots are of pale, long-haired brunette women with dark eyes. They're often pretty tall, too, framed around trees or fences or cars that make judging their height pretty easy. Bigger on bottom and smaller on top—

My heart slams into my throat. My stomach flips. I fit the description of the women Ben likes to photograph to a T. Like… like they are all based on me. Like this whole portfolio is a sign from Ryan that he hasn't forgotten me.

I shut my laptop, shoot up from the couch, and switch on the light. In the wash of fluorescents, all my fears abruptly seem stupid. What the hell am I thinking? There's no way that's true. Ryan is dead. I watched him die. He's not sending me messages from beyond the grave. I grab my phone and text Dana to ask if we can move this week's appointment up. After a brief hesitation, I add that I might need some extra support this semester. My face burns. One day of classes, and I'm already falling apart at the seams. I need to pull myself together before Heather comes home. She wasn't here when I had my first big breakdown, and I like having someone in my life who isn't waiting for me to crack. I scoop up my laptop and start to head for my room.

Keys scrape in the lock. I freeze then force myself to take a deep breath. Heather opens the door, and I roll my eyes internally at my needless panic.

"Hey," she says breathlessly, yanking her keys out of the door. "Good first day?"

I shrug. "You?"

"Decent." She holds up a folder I know means an assignment from the *Arkly* and grins. "Oh, the new photographer asked about you."

3

ASKING AROUND

MY HEART HAMMERS so loudly I can barely hear myself ask, "The new photographer?"

"Yeah, Ben something." Heather drops her keys on the hall table along with a small pile of envelopes, likely bills.

Oh, God. Oh, fuck. My feet move without my command, dragging me closer to Heather. Her blonde hair in its usual high ponytail shines in the summer sun. I try to focus on that, to ground myself. My ribs feel like they're caving in.

"What did he say?" I manage.

"Well, he thinks you're cute." Heather furrows her eyebrows and takes a step back. "He's helping out in one of your classes, right?"

Heather doesn't know about my institutionalization. She wasn't on campus yet. And, God, I'd like to keep it that way. I need one person on campus who knows me and doesn't look at me like I'm about to crack. *Deep breaths, Marcie.*

"Yes." I take another step back that I hope doesn't look robotic and drop my laptop on the table. "How did he find you?"

11

That seems to put her a little more at ease. She saunters into the kitchen and begins pulling out the kettle for tea. I watch her through the breakfast bar and try not to seem like I'm about to explode.

"Oh, he basically stumbled into the office in a daze, and Steph asked him," she says. "And then apparently Danny, which I couldn't explain with a gun to my head."

I nod. She needs to go faster. I need to be normal.

"Anyway, Steph and Danny told him I was your roommate, so he came to me." She pours water into the kettle, plugs it in, and turns around. "He wanted to know if you wanted to go out sometime."

Ben's hair is the same color as Ryan's. Ben's smile is the same smile as Ryan's. Ben has a million pictures of women who look exactly like me. Maybe Ryan survived, and he knows what I—"

"What did he say?" I blurt.

Heather raises a perfectly arched eyebrow. "That he wanted to go out."

"No, like exactly." I pick at the skin around my thumbnail where she can't see. Should I giggle? Normal girls giggle when a guy likes them. I force a laugh, and it comes out sounding like I'm insane.

"You know, I thought he was cute, but I didn't expect you to turn yourself inside out like this." Heather laughs and grabs another mug. "I'm making you chamomile. You need to chill."

She thinks I like him. Is that good? Should I correct her?

She turns back before I decide. "I don't remember exactly what he said, but he was really sweet. Kind of awkward. He barely met my eyes, and he started across the room to talk to me like three times before he actually made it."

Ryan was confident. He had no problem approaching people. But I haven't seen Ryan in six years.

Because Ryan is dead, the Dana-voice in my head reminds me.

I nod and pick up the mail to give my hands something other to do than tearing my hangnails to shreds. Magazine for Heather. Bill for me. Bill for Heather. And at the bottom of the pile, a piece of spam mail clearly bearing the name Lily Nelson. My heart skips a beat.

"He called me Marcie?" I ask. "Like, without fumbling?"

Heather blinks a few times. "Uh, yeah? Why? I think he got your name from the class list."

He called me Marcie. Not Lily. My heart rate starts to slow. When I finally got released from the institution and started rejoining the living world, I returned to just about a million messages across my various social media platforms. Condolences for Ryan, for being locked up. More than enough messages asking if I saw something that night that "drove me crazy." I ran into Dana's office on a day we didn't have an appointment, sobbing, and told her I couldn't be Lily Nelson anymore. I wanted to be dead. But Dana pointed out I could just delete my accounts and change my name. Starting fresh was often smart after a trauma. So I deleted everything, smashed my old phone, filed a bunch of paperwork, and left Lily in the past where she belonged.

I'm Marcie because Ryan only knew Lily.

The kettle pops. Heather pours two mugs of tea and sets them on the breakfast bar between us.

"So, should I tell him you're interested? It might be good for you to have a boyfriend. Get you out of the apartment a little more." Heather grins. "Oh, my God! You can double with Everett and me!"

"No," I say sharply.

Heather flinches back a little. "I thought—"

"I'm not interested." Even if he's not Ryan—and he's not, he can't be, it's not possible—I could never go out with Ben. I don't even know if I can see him again. "I never will be. Tell him to back off."

"Whoa." Heather fiddles with her teabag. "Should I, like, tell other people to stay away? Am I missing part of the story?"

If he's not Ryan, I don't want to ruin his life. I shake my head. "He just… gives me the creeps."

"Noted." She nods. "Maybe I'll warn Steph anyway. He did go up to her first. Did he, like, say anything or…?"

"I want to talk about something else." I gnaw on my lip. "Please."

"No problem. God, I'm sorry, I didn't realize." She shakes her head. "Trust me, I have plenty to talk about. So, you know how excited I was to work with Mrs. Mathers?"

I nod. She spent almost all summer gushing about the head editor of the *Arkly* and what a dream learning from her would be.

"Well, it turns out she fucking quit the week before classes started." Heather yanks the teabag out of her cup and drops it immediately in the trash. "So we've got this new guy, *Scott*." She says his name like it's poison. "He wants us to call him Mr. Daugherty, but there's no way I'm doing that."

"That bad already?" I ask, trying to hold onto the normalcy of this conversation instead of letting my mind wander.

"I can't even begin to explain." Heather rolls her eyes luxuriously. She's really good at it, somehow. "It's like he literally doesn't even see the writers. I got chucked this assignment, which I'm really fucking grateful for, but he took my photographer into his office to have a whole conversation about his 'angle' for the piece. Kel literally had to leave the meeting and come out and tell me the whole thing."

I grimace supportively and fiddle with my own tea. I only have to make a few listening noises for Heather to keep going, which is one of my favorite things about her. It's not that she doesn't care about me— I think she does, in her own way—but she's a nonstop conversation machine powered by "mm-hmms." After Scott, she tells me about the weird power dynamic between juniors and seniors on the paper, as well as how crazy it is to work with real adults for the first time. I don't mention that I've done that with my summer job at one of the cafes in town. Heather's parents help out with tuition, so she spent the summer volunteering with a few other kids on a paper they were writing, editing, and publishing themselves. The spam letter for Lily taunts me from the pile of discarded mail. My mom would probably help out with tuition if I asked her. But I cut her off with everyone else in the great phone-smashing. Marcie's parents are on a sailboat trip around the world with no cell reception. It's easier this way.

By the time Heather moves onto what her assignment actually is, I almost feel normal, and my tea is brutally over-steeped. I pull out the bag and lean over the breakfast bar to drop it in the trash next to hers. She smiles sheepishly.

"The universal Marcie signal for homework you really need to get to?"

I nod. "But I hope Scott pulls his head out of his ass soon."

"Thanks." She rolls her eyes again like she's not hopeful. "But, oh my God! I completely forgot. How was the first day of your first full semester?"

I wander over to the table where I left my laptop, turning the question over in my head. "Remains to be seen, I think."

4

───────

OVERREACTION

Marcie

Two weeks into the semester, I lay on my stomach on the couch, typing up a lab report on my most recent phlebotomy practice. The blood didn't make me sick nearly as much as it usually does, so I'm crossing my fingers that exposure really is dulling the intensity of the association. The week after Ryan's death, I got my period and tested the limits of how long a body really can go without getting toxic shock syndrome because even my own blood sent me spiraling. Totally ridiculous.

Just like my reaction to Ben. He really is a guest lecturer, and I'm a huge baby. I showed up to the second class shaking like a fucking Chihuahua only for there to be no sign of him. Just like every other class for the following two weeks. I've only barely seen him around campus. Ardent isn't exactly a small school, but it's not huge either, and I haven't been going out of my way to avoid the *Arkly* offices. Without the constant threat of him hanging over my head, my classes are a lot more manageable.

My phone vibrates insistently, reminding me I really have to leave for therapy now. I finish one last sentence and hop up. Phone, wallet, keys. I head out into the late afternoon sunshine and lock the door—then check it. I've decided that's fine. It's keeping my Ben stress in check or something. I just won't tell Dana.

Slipping in a single earbud, I head down the stairs. Bright pop music hammers into my skull, and I smile. I can still hear my surroundings, but it's enough to dampen my thoughts. I walk past the mailbox, and out onto the pale stone path that connects our not-quite-off-campus apartment to the rest of Ardent just in time to see Heather walking up it toward me.

"Hey!" She waves like I might not have noticed her. "Doctor's appointment?"

I nod. She doesn't need to know what kind of doctor. "Back in an hour or so."

She closes the distance and grabs my arm as I start to leave. "Really quick."

I freeze. This is normal. Normal friends touch each other. Maybe the whole Ben thing made us closer? Heather's basically my best friend, and a small part of me has always wanted her to think of me as a close friend too.

"Homecoming's not far off." She grins. "And obviously the Ardent Alligators are going to crush the Bears, so Everett's already planning a victory party at his place. You should really come!"

I swallow. I mostly know Everett as a hunk of muscle who serves some important role on the football team and whom Heather spends more time with than a girl as smart as her really should. He's not a bad guy or anything, just really… jock-y. And that's even before we get into how much I hate parties. I haven't really been to one since—

She squeezes my arm and stares at me pleadingly. "Please? We can celebrate your first month of success too."

"I'll think about it." I say because otherwise I'm going to be late for therapy.

She jumps up and down like I said I'll throw a parade for it. Way too excitable sometimes. At least she lets me go.

I race off campus to Dana's office building a few blocks away, thanking God for the millionth time that the only therapist who actually listened to me when I was institutionalized does private practice as well. I don't even have to face the panic of a car to get to her. I knock on her door, panting, and she opens it with a small smile.

"Lost track of time?" she asks.

"Heather did." I walk inside and take my usual position next to the arm of her long, dark leather couch that has the best pillow. "Sorry."

"It's all right. You're only a minute late." Dana picks up her notebook and sits down across from me as always. "I don't even have anyone after you, so we can get the minute back at the end."

I exhale with relief. Dana's small kind of dark office is one of the only places in the world I actually feel comfortable. It's the only place that's been the same since I was released five years ago.

"Last time," she says, "we were talking about that guest lecturer. Do you want to pick up there or talk about whatever happened with Heather?"

"Heather's fine." I wave the thought away.

"So then tell me about Ben." She leans forward. "Have you seen him?"

I pick at the fringe on the edge of the pillow. "Not really."

"Not really?" She purses her lips. "Was he in class?"

I shake my head. "Still no on that front."

"Are you still experiencing the anxiety spikes when you have to go?" She scribbles a few notes.

"Yeah," I admit. "I know it's a total overreaction but... it was so intense, you know? He's so much like Ryan. I don't know how to face him."

"But he's not Ryan," Dana says gently. "He's Ben."

"He's Ben," I repeat automatically.

She sighs. "Tell me what you mean by 'not really.'"

I grimace. Dana always sees right through me. "So I was getting coffee between classes."

She nods.

"And one of the coffeeshops on campus is better than the others. By a lot." My mouth waters just imagining the croissants at the Bean and Gone, much less the coffee. "I headed over there, and… Ben was sitting inside. With the new lead editor." I recognized him instantly from Heather's descriptions, which have been growing more and more vivid. He really did look like he would take a picture next to a lion pretending like he shot it but it would be someone else's kill.

"What did you do?" Dana pushes a lock of her red bob behind her ear.

"I watched." I wince. "Just for a little! They were right next to the window, and he was gesturing a lot and… and it reminded me of Ryan."

It was completely stupid. I knew it at the time. I didn't even go in to get coffee either, just stumbled to my next class half-asleep. But Ryan had a particular way of moving when he wanted to make a point, and—

Dana sighs and closes her notebook around her pen. "I don't have to say it, do I?"

I shake my head, hot with shame. "He's not Ryan."

"No, he's not." Dana shakes her head, and the red hair comes loose again. "Marcie, you're on track to graduate in the spring. You're on the cusp of a new life, an even bigger fresh start than changing your name. Do you really want to jeopardize that with these silly delusions?"

I shake my head furiously. There's nothing in the world I want less.

"Okay." Dana squeezes her closed notebook, and the diamond in her wedding ring catches the light. She doesn't have any personal pictures in her office, but I've often wondered about her spouse. She deserves someone wonderful. "Then tell me three things that make the two of them different."

Dana works me through exercises until the end of the appointment approaches. I'm feeling a lot more stable and even sillier about the coffeeshop thing than I did before walking in. It's beyond stupid. Ben's just some guy, and I'm not risking my health to seek him out anymore.

"Good," she says. "We're almost done for the day. Why don't we cool down by talking about what Heather had going on that made you late?"

I shrug. "Heather invited me to some homecoming party, but I'm not going."

"Why not?" Dana asks.

"I don't do well at parties." I fold myself around the pillow. "They remind me too much of…."

"Of prom?" she supplies.

I nod. The last time I saw Ryan alive. "And the drinking phase before I was institutionalized."

"Then I think you should go. Push yourself. Find out what you're really capable of."

Maybe it's just the warm, close walls of her office, but for the first time, the party actually kind of sounds like a good idea.

5

CHICKENING OUT

MARCIE

"I SWEAR to God you look hot," Heather says.

I adjust the minuscule dress she insisted on loaning me, looking at my reflection in her full-body mirror, and make a tepid attempt at believing her. The dress is charcoal-colored, rather than a full, show-stopping black. The mid-thigh hem does show off my legs. They're not nearly as good as they were during my theater days—the dancing in musicals helped, but standing up for that long was a huge contributor too. I'm taller than the average woman at 5'8, so my whole life has been filled with comments about how long my legs are. I guess they're decent. But the way the fabric clings just shows off how little I still have in the way of curves, and my hair looks like a wreck. No, Heather's just trying to be nice.

Another screaming cavalcade of frat boys thunders by outside, and I struggle not to flinch. I should never have agreed to this party. The game finished an hour ago with our victory, apparently, and Heather has spent the whole time since then getting ready—and getting me ready. As the hands on the clock tick closer and closer to when we're supposed to leave, I get more and more certain I'm not going.

"Heather—"

She turns around from where she's sitting at a little white makeup table. One eye is covered in complex shadow, and the other has a bare sweep of red. "Marcie. Do not tell me you're not going just because you're stressing about the dress."

"I'm not just stressing about the dress," I mumble as I wrap my arms around myself.

Her phone vibrates, like it has about a billion times since she got home. Just another reminder that Heather is going to have a ton of friends at this party, and I'm going to have kind of her. There's way, way more to stress about than the dress.

"Hey, are you actually freaking out?" She drops her usual high, fast tone, something like concern creeping into her voice.

My stomach turns. Great, now I'm the baby. "No. It's fine. Whatever."

She stands, crosses the room, and puts her hands on my shoulders. "Do you want to wear something else, or do you want me to tell you why you're hot?"

My face flames. "Neither. I want to stay home."

She shakes her head. "You're my friend, right?"

I shrug. Stupid. We're not in middle school anymore.

"You are," she says insistently. "And friends don't let friends turn into hermits when school gets tough. So, new dress or hotness?"

Her eyes scorch up into mine. Sometimes, I can really tell she used to be a cheerleader. She's going to make me confident enough to walk out that door if it kills her. Knowing me, it just might. But I sigh and ask for whatever the hell "hotness" is.

She spins me around by the shoulders. "Okay, I don't have to tell you your legs are crazy. But look how the straps show off your collarbone. And this color warms your skin right up so no one can tell you stayed inside all summer. And like, fuck, you might not be a perfect hourglass, but a fabric like this makes the absolute most of what you have. Add in the hair and makeup, and people will be falling all over themselves to meet *the new girl*." She waggles her eyebrows.

I get a little caught in the undertow of her excitement. The thin straps do show off more of my chest than usual, and I guess my collarbone does look good. I do look a little more alive. The fabric might be working for me. I offer her a small smile.

"The new girl?"

"Well, come on." She gestures at me. "Who's going to recognize Marcie in this? Especially if you let me do your makeup." She sticks out her lower lip pleadingly.

I look at myself one last time and heave a long sigh. "All right. My face is yours."

Heather claps.

MUSIC POURING out of the frat house Everett shares with his "brothers" hits my ears the second we turn onto the street. A few steps later, I recognize the crowd covering the lawn and spilling into the street. Someone sprints past us, shirtless, carrying a banner with a horrifying approximation of the alligator mascot and screaming wordlessly. I shrink out of their path into Heather. Fuck, this is so much worse than I thought it was going to be. Memories of the weeks immediately after I arrived at Ardent batter at me, blurry with alcohol.

"You're hot," Heather reminds me. "Mysterious new girl, right?"

I try to push some hair out of my face, but it's all up in what she called an "elegant sloppy bun," knocking me off kilter. At least I convinced her not to paint my nails so I can chew on them without poisoning myself. The late-summer heat sticks to my skin, and I want to crawl home. Instead, I nod. I need to do something that'll prove to Dana I can handle this semester, especially after the coffee shop incident.

"Good." Heather squeezes my hand and drags me closer to my doom.

We trudge up the front steps to a party somehow already in full swing. The bass of some awful song pounds into my skull, and eight people touch me before we even reach the door. There, a muscular frat boy puts up a hand to stop us.

"By declaration of the quarterback king of all time, Everett Beck —"

Heather clears her throat, and the frat boy actually looks down at us.

"Oh, shit!" he yells like we're not right in front of him. "Fucking sorry, dudes. Go right inside. Drinks on the left."

He shoves open the already mostly open door, letting loose another wave of sound, and gestures us inside.

"That's Justin," Heather shouts over the music as she pulls me inside. "Tight end, kind of a jackass, but he means well."

I nod. If tonight goes well, I'll never talk to Justin again.

"Oh, my God!" Heather squeals, immediately letting go of my hand to run over to a small cluster of girls in equally tiny dresses.

My heart hammers as I trail after her. She swore she'd introduce me to some people. Maybe these are them?

"—I know, right?" Heather says as I walk up, somehow already embedded in conversation. "Oh, before I forget, this is my roomie, Marcie! Take good care of her tonight girls, seriously."

I wave awkwardly.

"Intros, fuck." Heather grabs one of the other girls' cups and shoots whatever's inside, then grimaces. "God, you've got bad taste, Jules. Okay, this is Jules, Steph, and Alex."

The three of them wave. I've already forgotten which is which.

"Heather!" a voice booms across the party.

"Baby!" She turns with a grin.

Before I can even look for the source of the noise, Everett appears behind her and scoops her up. They spin for a second, kissing, and then he throws her over his shoulder.

"Sorry, ladies." He bows dramatically. "I need her."

As quick as he appeared, he disappears again, his hand on a

squirming Heather's ass. I blink a few times, then turn back to the women she introduced me to.

"So, uh... what are your majors?" I ask. I didn't used to bother talking at these things.

"What?" One of them, I think Alex, cups her hand around her ear.

"Majors!" I yell.

"Yeah, they're such a big deal," another one gushes. "Can you imagine dating a guy like Everett?"

I nod and slowly back away. They don't even notice. Not exactly my people. The beginning of a headache curls around my temples threateningly, and I spot a few folding tables end-to-end, covered in bottles of liquor. The drinks Justin mentioned. On my meds, I get drunk a lot faster than most people. One glass of wine with dinner is enough to knock me on my ass. But right now, being knocked on my ass would be a lot better than having a panic attack alone at a party. I walk over to the table.

Someone slams into my shoulder. I spin off course and turn, about to start shouting, but the fucking guy just keeps walking. I stare after him for a few seconds. He's bleach-pale, like he's never seen the sun before, but he has long, shaggy black hair and wears a black tank top and baggy black pants.

"You look like a goddamn cartoon character!" I shout, my nerves already fried.

He flips me off over his shoulder. I turn back to my path to the drinks. Yeah, blurring the edges of this place will make it a lot more tolerable.

6

HOMECOMING

Marcie

"Chug! Chug! Chug!" I shout with the rest of the crowd at some keg-standing someone or other. The red plastic cup in my hand is almost empty, which means it's time for a refill. My first. Or third?

The keg-standing person splutters foamy beer, and I cheer with everyone else. Who the fuck am I kidding? These parties are fucking great. I have to go to more. And the music is… is also great. I stumble away from the crowd, on the hunt for wherever the bar ran off to.

Something slams into my shins, and the room turns upside-down. I'm falling. Oh, shit! Before I can get my limbs together enough to catch myself, someone wraps warm arms around my waist and arrests my fall. I blink a few times and look up at my rescuer.

Blurry jaw. Blurry hair—not that long, maybe pink. Or purple? No, wait, that's the strobe lights, coloring his hair. Regardless, he's blurry-handsome, and I smile easily up at him from where I sit in what seems to be his lap.

"Did it hurt?" he asks.

I laugh. I could fall off a building right now and bounce, I think. "Not a bit!"

"No, uh." He shakes his head. "I mean when you fell, um—"

"I said no!" I adjust myself so I'm sitting up. Man, this couch is warm.

He smiles. "When you fell from heaven."

I throw my head back and laugh. Something about the booze and the cheesy pickup line and the blurry-handsome man is so completely, utterly perfect I feel like I'm floating away on a cloud of perfectness.

"So you've heard that one a time or two?" he asks.

I nod a few times. "I think Adam may have used it on Eve."

He smiles. I wonder if his blurry mouth is as warm as his arms. "All right, so it's been a little while since I've been to a party. Can you fault a guy? You fell into my arms."

"Sorry." I can't stop smiling. "But don't worry, I'm not too judgmental. This is kind of my first party."

"Really?" His pink-purple-blue eyebrows shoot up. "I'm surprised. You look so at home here."

I try to wave my empty cup and discover I've lost it. "Let's just say I'm very socially lubricated."

He laughs. "Maybe I should try things your way. I perform a lot better when a few close friends want to sit down for a game."

"Poker?" I nod seriously. "Or are you a proper old fogey, and when you say game you mean like, chess?"

"Hey, I'll have you know I've played board games that came out after at least 1995." He grins. "I'm pretty sure."

My next laugh surprises even me, less alcohol-fueled and more inspired by the easy banter between us. God, I forgot how much I like funny men. I forgot how much I like men! I can't even remember the last time I looked at one, and however blurry he might be, I am looking now.

"How did you escape your hermit cave in the mountains?" I ask. "Or was it more of a princess-in-a-tower situation?"

"Definitely princess tower." His blurry mouth twists wryly. "I'm a regular Princess Gwendivere."

My mouth drops open. "Gwendivere? Like from *Manticore Quest*?"

"No way! You know *Manticore Quest*?" He shakes his head, but I think he's smiling teasingly.

"What, women can't play video games?" I demand. "How very medieval of you."

He laughs. "Fuck no, but no one plays random German video games from defunct consoles. I swear, I thought it was just me and a dozen freaks on forum boards."

I pat his cheek. "You're not thinking broad enough, young warrior. The Internet is much bigger than forum boards. I've got whole websites of fan communities. I can show you"—I drop my voice into my best impression of Morgengraun, the witch from the game— "powers the likes of which you've never seen."

"Oof, that's awful." His whole body shakes with laughter. "And that's not even the fucking line."

"Yes, it is!" I smack his shoulder lightly. "I've only played it like a million times. Gwen's stuck over the cauldron, Sir Lancival isn't there yet, and she says the potion is going to grant her powers the likes of which you've never seen."

"So close." He leans back in mock pain. "But it's power the likes of which the world has never seen."

I laugh in disbelief. "The second person I meet in real life who knows this game is a fucking pedant! Not fair!"

"Totally fair." His smile catches the strobe as well, until he's all pink-purple-blue. "I'm basically saving your life. Now, you won't be humiliated on these many fan websites you brag about."

I shake my head and muster my itinerant thoughts to prove him completely, totally, ridiculously wrong.

Time turns to sand in my palms. I blink, and I'm facing the handsome stranger, now completely straddling his lap. Did I get back on him? No, the couch was warm. I never got back up. His arms are heavy and grounding around my waist, certain proof I'm not going anywhere, and he's got the most beautiful blue eyes I've ever seen.

"Lose your sentence?" he asks.

I was talking. Fuck. "Maybe. I think you might be too pretty to talk to."

"I get it, that's why I'm Gwendivere." He offers me a shy smile. "Someone really ought to hide me away to make sure my beauty doesn't go around messing up gorgeous women like yourself."

My face flames. He's flirting with me! I'm flirting with a strange man at a party, so strange I don't even know his name. I take a breath, wait for the anxiety to kick in, but I just drop my head against his shoulder in helpless laughter. I haven't given him my name either. This doesn't feel like a sloppy mistake. It feels silly, and wild, and free. Like I was told college was supposed to be.

"Ah, fuck, is that the time?" he mumbles.

I pull back off his shoulder to see him checking his phone with a frown. I can't quite put the numbers together enough to make a time, but it seems late. Or late enough that it has gotten early again.

"Why?" I ask. "Got somewhere else to be?"

He grimaces. "This is going to sound like bullshit."

"Don't worry, Gwendivere, I'll believe you." I wrap my arms around his neck and smile.

He sighs. "I'm expecting a call, and if I don't pick up, or if I take it from here, there's going to be hell to pay. I have to go."

I nod sagely. "Ah, the classic girlfriend in Canada excuse."

That startles a laugh out of him. "You really think I'm putting you off right now?"

"A mysterious call? A sudden excuse to leave?" I tighten my arms around his neck. "Either you've actually got a girlfriend, or you're trying to run away."

"No girlfriend; no running away." He meets my gaze. "Promise, okay?"

Well, who am I to disagree with a man who promises? I stare at his blurry mouth. It would be so easy to lean in. Only a few breaths separate us, and then I would know what he tasted like, if he really is as warm all over.

The room spins a little. Maybe I'm way too drunk for this. But tonight is not a night for giving up. I twist and snatch his phone out of his hands. With only a few incorrect clicks, I open his contacts and create a new one. My number goes on one line. Above it, I start typing "Marcie," then back up. I'm being silly and free. I type "Sir Lancival," then hit save and give his phone back.

"Is that what you want me to call you?" he asks with a smile.

I collect all my muscles and launch up off his lap as gracefully as I can manage. "Text me sometime and ask."

It's nearly a perfect exit. I stumble at the corner and almost collapse, but I don't look back to see if he was watching. I'm free. Dana's going to be so proud of me.

7

———

REPERCUSSIONS

Marcie

Someone is jackhammering my skull. Not only that, they're shining a search light right at my closed eyelids, trying to burn away my corneas before I've even really woken up. Someone wants me really, truly dead. I crack open an eye—fuck, it's so goddamn bright—and make out hazy, familiar shapes. That dark brownish lump could be my desk. The dark blue underneath me could be my bed, if I passed out on top of my comforter. The searchlight takes on the distinctive rectangular shape of my window. Everything hurts.

A warm, tempting smell winds through the air. Eggs. And bacon! My stomach rumbles. I grumble back at it. We'll be staying in bed until they turn the searchlight off, thanks.

My bladder also protests, and it's in a far less negotiable mood. With a great act of will, I sit up. My stomach lurches, but last night's drinks don't make a reappearance. Thank God for that. I'm still wearing Heather's dress. Achingly, eyes half-closed, I fumble through changing into sweatpants and a T-shirt, then reach for my phone on my nightstand before heading to the bathroom.

My hand meets bare wood. No phone. The charging cable hangs limply from its hook. Fuck. I paw through the discarded pile of clothes—I brought a purse, but Heather's dress did have pockets. Still nothing. If I left my phone at a frat house, I'm going to lose it. Of course, my bladder informs me it's going to lose it first, so I waddle out into the living room feeling like a zombie.

The warm smells intensify, and I spot Heather and Everett in the kitchen. They start to say something, but I wave them off. Bathroom first.

With my basic needs satisfied, and my teeth brushed to scare off some of the dead-person taste in there, I feel a little more human when I return to the living room.

"Morning." Heather scrambles some eggs, wearing nothing more than a sports bra that struggles to cover all of her chest and what looks like a pair of Everett's boxers, dangling perilously off her hips.

Everett flips me a lazy salute, his addition to the morning sludge-pile his shockingly muscular bare chest and a loose pair of Ardent sweatpants.

"What's that smell?" I ask.

"Hangover cure." Everett tends some kind of hash in a second pan. "Grease and more grease."

I groan and drop onto one of the stools at the breakfast bar. "Is anybody willing to take pity on someone who doesn't party?"

Heather laughs tiredly. "Course. We are making enough for three, and I was gonna come wake you soon. Did you have an okay time?"

"Yeah." I lean my crossed arms on the chipping counter, then put my aching head on them. "I think. From what I can remember."

Heather laughs. Everett slips an arm around her waist and kisses the side of her forehead. Normally, their PDA grosses me out, but aside from the new, painful body I've woken up in, everything bothers me a little less this morning.

"You like, disappeared," she says. "Any idea where you got off to?"

Everett dumps the hash from his pan into hers. "I think I saw you on a couch at one point?"

A few memories click back into place.

"God, I think I actually met someone." My voice rasps out of my throat. "If I could remember what he looked like."

"Ooh." Heather stirs the eggs a few more times then shuts off the heat and divvies the food onto three plates. "What do you remember?"

I accept my plate and walk with the two of them into the living room. They basically share one cushion of the couch, leaving me free to spread out on the other half. I take my first bite of the hangover cure and moan.

"You're gods," I say through a full mouth.

They laugh in unison.

"Come on. Tell us about the guy," Heather says.

"I remember he was funny." I smile between bites. "And easy to talk to."

She nods approvingly. "A sapient life form at a frat party? Shock of shocks."

I think about throwing a pillow at her, but that would take so much energy, so I just laugh with Everett.

"I didn't learn his name." I blush as I poke at my food. "But I gave him my number?"

"Oh, my God!" It's a downbeat version of Heather's usual squeal, but that's honestly much preferred at this time of day. "One party, and I'm turning you into a slut."

I shake my head. "We didn't do anything. I didn't even kiss him."

Heather boos. I laugh.

"Do you remember what he looked like?" Everett asks. "I might know him."

"His hair was… um…." I remember the strobe lights, his warmth. Absolutely nothing identifiable. "No? But he likes the same weird video game I like."

Ryan and I found *Manticore Quest* at the tiny thrift shop that survived for a couple months in our town one summer and played it ceaselessly. I wasn't kidding when I said I had way bigger fan communities, but the mystery man from last night is the first person I've met in real life who's also heard of it.

"I'll put up posters for frat-house missed connections." Everett grins.

Heather smacks him. "Don't be a dick. Seriously, I'm glad to see you coming out of your shell a little, Marcie. Has he texted you yet?"

I grimace. "I may have also lost my phone. Can you help me look after breakfast?"

The egg-whatever-it-was disappears quickly, and soon, we're all on our hands and knees, trying to guess what drunk-Marcie might've done.

"Aha!" Everett holds up the little black clutch I brought to the party triumphantly. "I have the bag. Cross your fingers for phone."

I scramble over to him and grab it. The zipper sticks a little, but I yank it open. Phone and wallet, still inside. Plus antacids, pain relievers, and a bunch of other things I probably should've taken last night. I ignore them all in favor of my phone. Right in the middle of the screen sits a single notification from an unknown number.

Hey, it's Gwendivere with the Canadian girlfriend. I broke up with her on the phone last night. Want to hang out sometime?

"Yes, he did!" I shove my phone at Heather.

"Inside jokes?" she asks

I nod

"Then make a date!" She grins at me.

I can't imagine doing anything else. I was right to be hopeful about this semester.

8

DATE NIGHT

Marcie

The following Tuesday, I breathe out slowly and stare at my open closet door. My clothes stare back at me, no more helpful than the last twelve times I've looked at them. My phone vibrates, and I dive for it instead.

Is it too lame to say I'm really looking forward to this?

I clutch the phone to my chest and try not to squeal. I feel like a kid, but my mystery man—it feels too weird to call him Gwendivere in my head, even though I already know I'll probably never change his name in my contacts—has been texting me all week, and my stomach fills with butterflies every time. It's a proper lying on my stomach and kicking up my heels crush. I can't remember the last time I felt like this.

Okay, I can, but I'm not thinking about *him* tonight. I open mystery man and I's message thread and text him back.

Don't worry. I'll slay the dragon of lameness for both of us. I'm looking forward to it too

The message doesn't even send me into a spiral, wondering if I've actually made everything so much lamer, or if he's going to think I'm making fun of him in a bad way, or if I just sound too ridiculous to go on a date with and he's going to cancel. Texting him has just been easy, like talking to him that night. Or what I remember of it, through the hangover. I don't think I actually blacked out, but my psychiatrist wasn't exaggerating about the effects of the meds. I really do have to be careful.

My phone vibrates again, and I check it to see a string of emojis. The blushing face, a sword, a dragon, and then a skull. I giggle and toss it back on the bed.

Heather leans into my open doorway. "Hey! Today's the day, right?"

I nod. "Just getting dressed now."

"Fuck, you look happy." She wanders in and sits on my bed. "I remember when Everett and I were like that. Don't get me wrong, I'm still beyond happy, but the first-date stuff is always so fun. You need help picking out an outfit?"

I bite my lip as I look at my closet again. Nothing jumps out at me, but I remember Heather and Everett's first date. He took her to a club someone in his family owned, or knew the owner of, and Heather wore a dress so short she made me watch her bend over before she left to make sure she wasn't showing her whole ass. Apparently, a little bit of ass was fine. Since my mystery man and I have already done the drunken, half-dressed thing, we agreed on a much more normal evening coffee date at Bean and Gone. As supportive as Heather has been this past week, I don't know that her tastes are going to be super helpful to me tonight.

"Uh...."

She laughs. "Loud and clear. I'm going to go do homework. Let me know if you need help with makeup or hair or anything."

I nod, and she leaves me alone with my closet. Lots of grays and browns jump out at me. The occasional blue or black. Blending into the background clothes. Tonight, I want to be myself, but I want to be Lancival too. I want to be the fearless woman I was when I met him.

And coffee isn't exactly going to get me there, no matter how sensitive my meds are.

A memory floats through my mind. This past summer, Heather dragged me shopping with her in Arlington. I basically just carried her bags and told her she looked cute, which prompted her to compare me to Everett but was more fun than I would have expected–until the very end. We went into this last tiny boutique, and a rack in the corner labeled "Tall Girls" caught my eye. I'm no basketball player, but I'm tall enough that most shorts and skirts are uncomfortably short or just awkward. While Heather browsed, I drifted over and pulled a baby-blue romper in my size. Of course, as soon as I touched something, we weren't leaving the store until I bought it. I haven't even touched it since I put it away, but it's not too hard to find in the back of my closet. With a little bit of wriggling, I slid it on.

Just like in the store, it fits perfectly. The feminine flounce at the neckline makes it kind of look like I have boobs worth noticing, and the shorts don't pinch or hit at the dreaded mom-short length. I might actually look cute. I twist in the mirror a couple of times. *Okay, yeah. I can wear this.*

Still, I check the weather. It's in the seventies currently, but it'll be mid-sixties by 8:00. I should layer, just to be safe. I pull a comfortable brown cardigan from my sweater shelf, grab my ancient pair of canvas sneakers, and feel a little more like myself. Just an updated version of myself. Exactly what I'm looking for. With a little lip gloss and mascara, I'm ready to go.

I walk out to find Heather in the living room, tapping away on her laptop. She glances up.

"Gorgeous," she declares. "Can I just do one thing to your hair?"

I check my phone. We agreed to meet at 7:00, which is in half an hour. It'll take me five minutes to walk to Bean and Gone if I rush, ten if I don't, plus a line to get a drink—

"Sure," I say.

She leaps up with a grin and rushes to her room. When she returns, she holds a bulky, tortoiseshell clip in her hand. I eye it warily.

"Trust me." She spins me around by my shoulders and scrapes the front of my hair back, then pins it with the clip. With a small hum, she pulls a couple strands of hair out from the clip to hang in front of my face, then holds up her phone in selfie mode so I can see.

Me–but upgraded. Way better than my usual ponytail.

"Thank you," I say earnestly.

"Any time." She flops back onto the couch. "Just text if you need the living room clear when you're coming home, and hang a sock on the door."

My face flames. "It's a coffee date!"

Her laughter chases me out of the apartment. I lock the door, put my keys in my purse, and stop myself from checking the lock. Heather's home. I'm upgraded. I can do this.

It takes me three minutes to walk to Bean and Gone. I didn't just walk quickly, I rushed. I duck behind a tree and flap my cardigan a few times to release any smells of perspiration. *Chill, Marcie.*

Easier said than done. I walk inside to find no line at all, order my usual americano misto—an americano made with half cream, half water—and find a table near the back of the café, away from the counter, all before the clock hits 6:45. I hope he doesn't think I'm lame for arriving so early, but part of me already knows he won't. If I was going to scare him off with how excited I am, I would have by now. I sip my coffee then pull out my phone and text him where I am. It's not like I can hide. In my memories, he doesn't seem as drunk as I was, so he might actually know what I look like. I bounce my foot and watch the door. Pair of freshmen. Pack of sorority sisters. *No, no, no.*

The door opens, and my lungs shrivel as Ben walks in.

9

———

MISTAKE

MARCIE

No. No, no, no. I didn't spend a whole night talking to Ben. I didn't spend all week texting Ben! My breath races. My heart hammers. He can't be Ryan because… because….

Ben catches my eye and smiles. He's wearing a pair of jeans so crisp I have to assume he ironed them before leaving the house and a short-sleeved button-down with a tiny print I can't make out from here. *Oh, fuck, he's walking over.* I shove one of my hands beneath the table and squeeze it into a fist so tight, bright crescents of pain spark through my system as my nails dig in.

"My dear Lancival." He half-bows as he approaches. "I should've known you'd beat me here. Do you mind waiting while I get my drink?"

I shake my head. He can't be Ryan. He just can't be. I watched Ryan die, even if I didn't know that until his mom told me the next day. I went to his funeral. But oh, God, he looks so much like Ryan.

He turns away and joins the still-short line. I stare at his back. He

43

holds his shoulders like Ryan did. I think. At this point, I could be making all of this up.

I could be making this up! But I finally have a live sample of Ben to compare to the pictures of Ryan on my phone. I can finally prove that my mind is playing tricks on me. Below the lip of the table, I unlock the screen and click on the gallery.

The folder of Ryan photos doesn't pop up. That happens sometimes. My phone likes to hide my hidden folders. But when I click on the button that should reveal all my folders to me, it isn't there either.

My heartbeat in my ears starts to sound like a war drum, like a call to action. I search my whole phone. Not even a single instance of his name, but I guess that's not weird. Did I move them to my laptop? I was definitely on my laptop last time I stalked Ben.

And you lost your phone after the party, an awful voice in my head reminds me.

I inhale. I didn't really lose my phone.

I exhale. I found it under the couch.

I inhale. If someone deleted the pictures off my phone, it couldn't have been Ben. It would've had to be someone I came home with. Which would be much more comforting if I remembered getting home.

My ribs threaten to cave in, collapsing my lungs forever. I choke on the exhale.

Ben returns to the table with a wide-mouthed latte mug in his hands. "Don't make fun of me, but I think I've had enough of these caramel lattes that they may have replaced my blood by now."

It's like a break in the clouds. Ryan hated sweet coffee. He took his black, or when he'd just pulled an all-nighter, with a shot of espresso. I don't need the pictures. I can prove they're different in a million ways.

"I don't mind." I force a smile. "One of my friends used to make fun of me for putting one sugar in my americano."

"Oof." Ben grimaces playfully. "Sounds like a real hard ass. Let me guess, she always suggested French films when you watched movies?"

Ryan was the one who made fun of me. Another strike against

Ben. And maybe a third for the dig at French films. They weren't Ryan's favorite by any means, but he believed directors should watch movies from across the globe if they really wanted to call themselves masters of their craft.

"Sometimes." I sip my coffee. "So, I don't know if you noticed, but I was a little out of it last Saturday."

Ben smiles. "A little? I was surprised you woke up to text me back."

"I'm kind of a lightweight," I say carefully. "But I figured it was time to admit that if we did any of the getting-to-know-you questions, I don't remember."

"Not unless you count deep *Manticore Quest* discussions as getting to know you." He leans back in his chair and runs a hand through the flop of sandy hair that nearly falls into his eyes. "I don't think we even exchanged names. I'm Ben, if you don't remember from class."

"I remember." My tongue is made of lead. I couldn't forget him if I wanted to. "Um, Marcie."

"I remember too." He smiles conspiratorially. "It's a unique name. Where does it come from?"

It was the first thing that popped up on a random name generator when I was filling out my name-change paperwork. "It was my dad's mom's name. She passed a few months before I was born."

"That's sweet," he says. "I have no idea who I'm named after, but I used to tell people it was Benjamin Franklin."

Ryan would know I was lying. So I allow myself the luxury of actually raising my eyebrow in surprise at Ben's admission.

"Why him?"

He laughs. "I really keep hitting my lamest stories. Okay, so imagine you're Ben A., you're about seven, and you want something to distinguish you from Ben C., Ben H., and Ben S."

I nod.

"And then imagine you learn about Benjamin Franklin and all his great work in Philadelphia, and you know your parents moved from New Philadelphia right before you started school." He laughs self-consciously. "Drop the 'new,' and you're ready to start telling people you're one of his direct descendants."

I smile. It's easy to picture him young—easy because I knew Ryan at that age—and the story is so unique. Ryan never had anything like that.

"You can laugh." He gestures broadly. "It's my mom's favorite Ben-as-a-kid anecdote. I must've heard it a thousand times."

"I understand that." I nod like I've spoken to my mom in the five years since my institutionalization. "Are you close then?"

His smile grows a little tight. "We spent a lot of time together. I went to college close enough to home to live there. This is my first real jump out of the nest."

"I can barely tell." I offer him a smile in turn. Ryan's mom was protective, but that was at least partially because it was just the two of them. "Where is home, then?"

"Galesburg, Illinois. Proper flyover stuff, far from this bustling eastern seaport." He grins. A college town sprouted up around Ardent, and we're not far from D.C., but it's far from bustling. "What about you?"

"Aurora, Indiana, so I get you." I sip my coffee and watch his expression. Aurora has been my go-to fake hometown for years now, just a fifteen-minute drive from Dillsboro, where I actually grew up. Where Ryan and I grew up together.

Ben nods. "I think I might've actually heard of that. Isn't it really picturesque?"

There's not a flicker of disbelief or hesitation. "Uh, yeah."

"Sorry, I know not everything's a photograph waiting to happen." He ducks his head. "I'll step out from behind the lens, promise. Tell me what it's actually like."

He leans forward like he's genuinely curious. There's a sparkle in his blue eyes that Ryan only had when he was completely invested in a project, his forget-to-sleep-for-three-days look. But Ben seems much more at ease. I swallow.

"Picture what people in bustling East Coast cities think looks quaintly Midwestern, and you've pretty much got it."

He closes his eyes and nods seriously. "Mm-hmm. Picturing."

I stare at him for a second. Heather said he was nervous. The man in front of me is a little awkward, sure, but nervous?

A smile creeps across his lips, and he opens one eye. "Am I still picturing?"

I laugh, and a little of the tension slips out of my shoulders.

1 0

———

CLOSING TIME

MARCIE

I THROW MY HEAD BACK, my sides aching from how hard I've been laughing.

"I knew you wouldn't believe me!" Ben says. "I warned you!"

"You said she bit you!" I splutter between giggles. "A real, adult, *adult* model!"

"She didn't understand that I was a real photographer, not a set-up for a scene." He laughs with me in a rumbling baritone I wish I could bottle.

"Hi, uh, sorry to interrupt."

I close my mouth around the last of my laughter and open my eyes to see Anaya, one of the baristas who I've had a few classes with, standing next to our table.

"Are we being too loud?" My face burns. "We can keep it down."

She shakes her head. "I came to let you know we're closing up for the night. You don't have to go home, but you can't stay here and all." She puts a check on our table and walks away.

I blink a few times then pick up my cup of coffee and sip it to clear my head. I must've misheard her. But my coffee is ice cold. And she gave us a check for the pastries that used to occupy the crumb-covered plate between us. Pastries we ordered together, off the triangular menu on the table I haven't touched in my six years at Ardent.

Ben rubs the back of his neck. "Sorry, I didn't mean to keep you out so late."

I check my phone, and my stomach flips. It's eleven o'clock. I spent four hours in this café with Ben without even noticing. Heather even texted to make sure things were going well. I look at him, and my stomach does a double back-handspring. That's Ryan's sheepish smile, mostly reserved for parents and teachers. I was supposed to be testing Ben, figuring him out, but I barely know anything more than I did before I sat down. A few stories. A childhood he claims happened in Illinois. Easy lies.

"I'll pay." He reaches for his wallet. "If you don't mind. I know it's not modern, but I'd really like to."

I open and close my mouth a few times. He seems to take that as agreement and pulls out a wad of bills. Okay, not a suspicious wad of bills. More like a bunch of fives and ones around a twenty or two. But it's weird that he's paying in cash at all, in this day and age.

My mouth won't obey my requests to comment on this.

Anaya reappears to take the check and disappears again. I survey the table. A twisted napkin bears witness to my attempt to make a rose out of it like I used to be able to. Ben has a second cup, but I still only have one. Four hours.

He wipes his hands on his pants, drops a couple extra dollars on the table as a tip, and stands. "Did you walk or bike?"

"Walk," I answer automatically.

His glowing smile warns me I've made a mistake before he says anything.

"Can I walk you home?"

I tug on the sleeve of my cardigan, the bright red nail marks in my palm from when he walked in still stinging. If he were Ryan, in four hours, I'd surely have spotted something that gave him away. I couldn't have coffee with my dead best friend and not notice. Right?

The little Dana in my head agrees. I'm letting Ryan hold me back again, indulging in delusion.

Ben holds a hand out for me to take, and my heart slams against my ribs. Even if I assume he's not Ryan, he's a stranger. A stranger who just moved here and asked about me after only one class. It would be really crazy to tell him where I live.

"Alas, my Lady Gwendivere," I say, "it is for the knight to walk the princess home, not the other way around."

Ben laughs. "You've got me there. All right, if you're sure you're not going to get too cold doing both."

I gesture to the cardigan. He lets his hand fall without saying anything, and we walk out into the night air.

"Jesus, the temperature really does drop at night here." He shivers.

"And you were worried about me getting cold." I smile wanly.

"You're already used to it." He shakes his head. "I'm used to it being cold all day and all night. Nice and predictable."

"You'll get used to it." I bite my lip. "I mean, if you stay. Are you staying?"

He shrugs and stuffs his hands into his pockets. "Depends how this first year goes. Technically, I'm on probation."

"Is this what you want to do with your life?" I gesture at the campus. "The teaching thing?"

"Nah, it was just an opportunity that came up. And my mom likes the idea of me teaching." He stares ahead. "I'd like to do the impossible."

"What's that?" I find myself asking against my better instincts.

He waggles his eyebrows. "Make art."

That startles a laugh out of me. "You're a photographer; it can't be that hard."

"You'd be surprised." He shakes his head. "Most of the gigs are commercial, like ads and stuff, weddings, or somebody's really specific fetish."

"But you have such a specific portfolio online."

He raises an eyebrow, and I realize my mistake. My heart races, and my face burns.

"That sounds—I mean—"

"Did you look me up?" he asks quietly.

"No!" I blurt. "Maybe."

There's a beat of painful silence, filled only by my pounding pulse. This is it. If all of my worst fears are right, he's about to pull out a gun and kill me for, I don't know, failing to pull him out of the way of the car. If I'm wrong, I'm just a moron who ruined my first kind of nice date in six years.

Ben laughs. "I looked you up too."

The relief that courses through my system makes me a little weak in the knees, and he catches my arm when I stumble.

"Hey, I thought Lancival did the saving," he says.

I smile up at him. "It's a role reversal."

The rest of the walk to his apartment, another not-quite-off-campus one in a different block than mine, passes quickly. I don't think too much about the time, the darkness, the fact he hasn't let go of my arm. I do study his building when we arrive, but it's the same featureless block as every other. We stop in a pool of lamplight, and I nudge a rock on the ground. How do we do the goodbyes? Do I hug him? Shake his hand?

"I had a really nice time tonight," Ben says.

Like something out of a movie, he leans in to kiss me. Every muscle in my body locks. What if I'm right? What if I'm wrong, and he has something else awful to hide? I haven't exactly set the standard for honesty tonight. What if—"

His mouth touches mine. It's feather-light, delicate, testing. He doesn't even grab me, like he's making sure I can leave. My own body keeps me here, but the screaming alarm in my head is ever so slightly drowned out by the faint taste of cinnamon on his lips. He kisses me again, like my stillness is encouragement. I inhale his breath.

Ryan—*Ben* leans back. I blink. I never kissed Ryan, except in a few dreams I promptly shoved back into my brain and forgot about. I have nothing to compare to.

"I'll text you." He kisses my cheek and walks inside.

I stand on the sidewalk, stupidly, for several minutes before turning and racing home.

11

CONFESSION

EVERY RUSTLE in the bushes or shifting shadow makes me jump. When I finally reach the door, my fingers shake around the keys. My lips buzz like they're reminding me of what just happened, making it impossible to forget. I just kissed Ben. Ben just kissed me. And I still don't know if I'm crazy, or he's exactly like Ryan.

When I finally force the door open, Heather twists around on the couch.

"Holy shit! Text next time, okay?" she says. "I thought you were getting ax-murdered or something."

I take a deep breath. I've really enjoyed having someone in my life who doesn't look at me like I'm crazy. That's at least half the reason I stopped living with my assigned roommate from freshman year. That, and her weird obsession with cabbage. But Heather is the only friendly face inside the mile or so to Dana's office, and I feel like I'm about to rattle out of my skin. I close the door behind me, and the dam breaks.

"My best friend in high school was named Ryan Evers." Oh, God, I haven't said his name since I told it to Dana back in inpatient. My stomach lurches.

"O...kay?" Heather sits up. "You seem messed up. Come sit, and I'll make tea."

I shake my head, following her instructions anyway. I can't sit until I stop vibrating.

"We had another best friend, Theresa, and—and she doesn't matter to this story, so I'm going to focus. Cool. Thanks." I pace behind the back of the couch. "Ryan died. Senior year. Car accident." I can't say anything more than that without my whole stomach pushing itself out through my mouth. Even that much burns like acid.

"Fuck, I'm sorry." Heather offers me her hand for comfort.

Ben's hand in the restaurant flashes over it in my mind's eye. I ignore the gesture. Still pacing. Totally normal.

"We both wanted to go here," I say. "He was going to be a director, and I was going to be an actor. Maybe in his films; maybe not." I turn to her with a wild smile. "I loved dancing. Can you believe that?"

"You have the body for it." She bites her lip. "Can I get you water? Did you take something? If we go to the hospital, they won't—"

"No hospital!" I shout. The rest of her words filter back in. "Sorry. No, I haven't taken anything. I'm just stressed, and I started in the wrong part of the story. Um, my date tonight? Ben."

Her mouth falls open. "Creepy Ben? No!"

I nod. "But also I told you he was creepy because, hey, remember dead best friend Ryan? Well, Ben's the fucking spitting image of Ryan. Face, hair, gestures, everything." I drop over the back of the couch, sitting upside down next to Heather as the confession slips past my lips. "Everything."

"That's crazy." She brushes hair out of my face.

The vibration starts to slow. I laugh. "You don't know the half of it."

"Tell me." She closes her laptop and sets it aside. "I always flunk my first paper back anyway."

Tears bead in my eyes. *Holy shit, I'm so stupid.* How did I let myself end up here?

"I tried to come here without Ryan," I whisper.

"And you did." She smiles. "That's impressive, after what you went through."

I shake my head. "It's really not. I… spun out. I was seeing him everywhere." I put up my hand to stop what I assume will be her banal platitude about everybody feeling like that when they lose someone. "Not like… a glimpse in a crowd. Like, everywhere. And then I started partying because that's what you do in college." I shake my head. "I don't know what did it, but before Thanksgiving, I wasn't just seeing him, I was talking to him. Inviting him to parties, helping him with his homework. Someone reported me, and I spent the next six months in the Harvey Howard Hospital."

Heather mouths the name, and I watch the lightbulb go off in her mind. "You got sent to a mental hospital?"

"Full psychotic break." I smile grimly. "And now, here's Ben, and I don't have any pictures of Ryan to prove that my brain is just making up that they look exactly the same, but even if I could prove that, I don't know if I want to, because that would mean I'm crazy again." A tear slips down my cheek.

Silence wraps cold fingers around me. I close my eyes. This would be the part where Heather responds, but she's obviously deciding how to explain to the housing office why she can't live with me anymore. A slide of fabric on fabric reaches my ears, and I feel Heather's warm leg against mine. When I open my eyes, she's upside-down on the couch next to me. There's worry in her gaze, but thank fuck, no pity.

"One of my friends in high school killed herself," she murmurs. "It's not the same, obviously, but I'm not going to, like, freak out because of that. I've been through it before, and it sucks."

With how bouncy she is… God, it sounds awful, but I just kind of assumed her life was basically easy. I never would've guessed.

"With that out of the way, I've gotta ask a couple questions." She smiles ruefully. "You're still going to therapy right? And taking whatever meds you have?"

I nod.

"Great." She takes my hand. "Then as far as I see things, there's only one option here."

"I'd love to have only one option."

"You have to stop seeing Ben," she says. "Either there's some batshit conspiracy going on, and you don't want to end up in the middle of it, or more likely, he triggers something you don't need triggered. There are, like, a billion eligible guys on campus. We'll find you another one." She squeezes my hand.

"That makes sense," I say.

Of course, it makes sense. Now that she's said it, it sounds like the most obvious solution in the world. I'll just avoid Ben. Block his number, ignore him in class, whatever it takes. Everything Dana and I have ever worked on tells me this is a completely unnecessary risk.

My lips start vibrating again, but I'm not going to make life decisions based on just my lips.

"Good." She smiles. "Then give me your phone."

"What?"

"I want to block his number and download a couple dating apps for you." She wiggles her fingers. "They're way more fun with friends, promise."

That, too, makes sense. And Heather is basically the most normal person I know, so I should follow her lead on this. I pull my phone out of the purse trapped under my body and hand it over.

Setting up the profiles requires moving for a quick photoshoot after Heather declares all the pictures I have "not proof of my hotness," and she helps me with a bio that hopefully doesn't make me sound as pathetic as I am. Or maybe "introvert looking for someone to lie around with" is just dating-app for pathetic, and the trick is on other people. Then, the swiping begins.

"He likes your favorite book," Heather says.

I shake my head. "He's got those veiny muscles. They make me think about drawing blood too much. Next."

Next. Next. The guys with blond hair and blue eyes still look too much like Ryan. The guys that pose shirtless scream "misogynist." The guys that pose with half-unbuttoned shirts and books scream "misogynist in disguise." We even find one guy who would normally be exactly my type, a homebody who's not too muscular or too pretty. I stare at him for a few seconds, willing something to come to life and make me want to go out with him. Nothing.

"They refresh all the time." Heather tosses my phone aside, formally giving up. "We'll find someone. Promise."

She gives me a hug, and I ignore the faint scent of cinnamon stuck to the inside of my nose.

12

ONE MINUTE AFTER MIDNIGHT

BEN

I ʀᴜʙ my eyes and adjust the color grade on the action shot I snapped during the last football game by another degree. It's so close, but it's not quite right. This is a front-page photo. Scott said so when he saw it on my damn camera. I should've done this before I went out with Marcie.

Despite my frustration, just thinking about her brings a smile to my face. Sure, I don't really have many first dates to judge it against—I think—but that seemed like a pretty good first date. A pretty great one. When I kissed her, she just melted, and I got the first sense she was as nervous as me.

God, I hope she couldn't tell how nervous I was.

I'll just text her. Something cute. Low pressure, but trying to see if she wants to go out again.

Yeah, like I know how to do that. I sigh and pick up my phone anyway. Hopefully, high pressure with a few nerdy references still gets the job done.

My stomach drops as I look at the screen. It's 12:01. A minute after I'm supposed to call Mom. My fingers slide, suddenly sweat-slicked, as I fumble through opening my phone and dial quickly.

She picks up before the first ring ends. "Benjamin. I thought you'd forgotten about me."

"Never, Mom." I save the image and wheel back from my desk. I can't work while on the phone with her. She'll know. "Just got wrapped up in some photo editing."

She hums distrustfully. "What's the picture of?"

"A football game," I answer automatically. "I caught this great shot with one of our linebackers in the air about to connect with their quarterback. Really dynamic, but I had the flash settings wrong, so the color needs a lot of work."

"Well, that sounds good." Mom's not much for emotion in her words, but I know her well enough to read the relief in her near monotone. She has me call her every night at midnight because she's terrified I'm going to let the "college party atmosphere" distract me from my work.

Or so she says. I think it's because this is the first time I've ever lived away from home, and she doesn't want me to stop thinking about her. On my more generous days, I even think that might be because she still loves me, and not because she's so terrified she hasn't left the house since—

"I'd like a copy of that, Benjamin," she says. "Uncle Andrew's birthday is coming up, and I think he would enjoy hanging it in his den."

I cast back through the endless list of names Mom calls family, friends blending with actual relatives in my mind. "Uncle Andrew is… Aunt Diane's husband?"

"No," Mom says sharply. "Aunt Diane… moved years ago, and hearing her name is quite painful for me. Uncle Andrew is a confirmed bachelor."

I mark Aunt Diane "deceased" in my mental records. I don't think I ever even met the woman, so it's no great loss. "I'll send you a print as soon as I nail this color grade."

"It is good you take such pride in your work, even at a job like this." Mom makes a sound I know means she's sucking air through her teeth, a habit I always hated. It's only barely less teeth-grinding over the phone. "I know you're branching out, Benjamin, but I wish you'd consider my offer."

I sigh. "Mom, being pretty sure someone you know is about to open a gallery in Galesburg and would probably want to show my work isn't an offer; it's a pipe dream."

She clicks her tongue. "I wish you wouldn't use words like that either. They evoke drugs, and you don't want people getting the wrong idea."

I run my hand through my hair, feeling the texture underneath. I don't know if I care about *people* getting the wrong idea, but *person*? I picture Marcie's glowing dark eyes that first night on the couch, the way that glow flickered and threatened to die when I said I had to leave. Mom's right. I can't be too careful.

God, I wish she was right less often. It'd make moving away and resenting her phone calls way easier.

"Will do," I say. "How are things back home?"

She spits out a few rapid-fire anecdotes. Mom has the craziest ability to strip the humor out of even the funniest stories. I make it through one about a woman that apparently used to coach my soccer team throwing eggs at her husband during a town meeting without cracking a smile.

"And you, Benjamin?" she asks.

The story of my date with Marcie tempts me. It's too perfect that we kept running into each other, and I'm thrilled she agreed to go out with me, especially after her roommate yelled at me for being a creep at work.

Then, I remember Rebecca.

My first real girlfriend was a friend of a friend who shared a couple of classes with me our sophomore year of college. She took pity on a poor, hapless loser by actually asking me out. For the first three dates, I could barely string a sentence together. Not that I was that different on non-date outings back then. She put up with me, let me get my sea legs with girls, because she "found my attempts charming." Everything was going great until I invited her back to my house for Sunday dinner one weekend. Mom took an instant dislike to her. Thus began the campaign of thorns. There's nothing else to call it. Every time Rebecca came over, every time they ran into each other at school events, Mom chipped away at her. Every time she came up in conversation between the two of us, Mom "just couldn't help" mentioning that she pictured me with someone different. Shorter, blonder, smarter, more focused. Our relationship lasted six months after that Sunday dinner, and Rebecca broke up with me tearfully, saying she just couldn't put up with Mom anymore.

Ditto with Leslie after that, though she only lasted three months. And then there was the two weeks of Christina.

Now, I know better. I just don't tell Mom about anyone I'm going out with, and we're all happy.

"Work's good," I answer.

"You know how I feel about vagaries, Benjamin." She sighs. "They're not good for either of us. Who's your favorite coworker?"

"Mr. Daugherty," I say immediately. "I mean, he's my boss, but he's really taken me under his wing." I laugh. "And he told me to call him Scott."

The grouchy-looking editor scared me at first, but the second he got me into his office, he turned into a whole different guy. Warm, friendly, encouraging. Working under him is going to be a dream.

"That's wonderful." Mom's voice actually contains a hint of warmth. "A boss is always a good person to be close to. Lean on him, learn from him, and you'll leave this place with valuable lessons."

"Maybe I'll ask him about this color grade," I say, half to myself.

"Smart." I can picture her nodding on the other end of the line. "An experienced eye will be able to see what yours can't."

Is she talking about herself?

"Well, it's twelve-thirty." She sighs. "Good night, Benjamin. Please try to call me on time tomorrow."

I say goodbye and hang up. After staring at my phone until nearly one-thirty, I decide against texting Marcie.

After all, I can just say something when I see her tomorrow.

13

BEAUTIFUL

MARCIE

THE SUN SHINES down on my shoulders as I march along the path to class the morning after my date with Ben. Bright and warm. Just like I'm going to be.

Because he's going to be in class today.

After weeks of avoiding the photography syllabus like it's a snake, I finally took a look last night. Each Ben-class is marked with a little asterisk, like an inescapable black hole.

I then checked Professor Washington's dictatorial attendance policy. "Expedition" classes, which all of Ben's are, can only be missed once a semester before you just fail.

So, I adjust my backpack and practice my smile. I'm totally, completely normal. I went on a bad first date last night. Half the campus probably did. And at least half of those people have to face their bad-date-ee in class today. Statistically, I wouldn't even stand out on a graph.

I freeze at the doorway to the classroom. Ben leans over one of the desks, fiddling with something in a black bag. A camera bag. Nothing scary.

My heart crashes against my ribcage.

Inhale. He grew up in Illinois.

Exhale. He has both his parents.

Inhale. He can't tell when I'm lying.

Exhale. He's not Ryan—because Ryan is dead.

I march into the room with my head held high, dedicatedly not thinking about the fact that I searched my whole phone for the pictures of Ryan after Heather went to bed last night and didn't find them. I'm clumsy when I'm drunk, obviously. Maybe I deleted them.

The thought makes my eyes sting with tears. I blink them away and sit just as the last student scoots in the door—I was barely on time, for once. Professor Washington closes it behind him.

"Well, we've only got an hour and a half, so I don't want to waste time," she says. "You all remember Ben Andrews?"

People around me nod. I stare at my notebook. I can't meet Ben's eye.

"Wonderful. Then I cede the class to him!" She sits with a flourish in the front row.

Ben clears his throat. "Uh, hi. This'll be the first class I've actually taught, if you can use that word, so take pity on me."

The kid in front of me snickers. I can barely hear it over my heart-beat. *Not Ryan. Not Ryan. Not Ryan.*

"For starters, as good as editing software and rules of composition are, nothing teaches faster than experience. You guys need to get out there and actually take the pictures you've been learning about!" He laughs awkwardly.

No one else joins in. Especially me. I scribble on the front of my notebook, half-listening.

"Right." He clears his throat. "All that to say, we're doing a mini-expedition to the quad to whet your whistles. Live models in settings where you can't control the light. If you want to do this profession-ally, that's going to be your bread and butter, so it's good to get used to it now. Pair up, and we'll head outside."

Everyone starts talking, and I pick my head up. What's happening? People are out of their seats, chatting, comparing cameras, pairing off. I play back the last few seconds in my mind, and my ribs squeeze.

Partners. He said partners. And I've been staring at my books since the class started, so if there's an uneven number—

"Looks like you're with me, um, Ms. Holt," Ben says.

I freeze. This can't be happening.

"You'll be editing your photos, too," Professor Washington calls over the chaos. "Remember what we talked about!"

Something warm unfolds in my gut, cutting through the ice. If we're editing our pictures, making extra copies will be easy. Which means I'm two steps away from having a real photo of Ben that I can use, just as soon as I find those pictures of Ryan.

If indulging in the delusion a little makes it go away forever, maybe it's not so bad. I bounce out of my seat and bound over to Ben.

"Hey." He smiles sheepishly. "I swear I didn't do this on purpose."

That hadn't even crossed my mind. Before worry can wrap icy fingers around my throat, I blurt out the first thing that comes to mind. "I've never actually taken a picture with this camera before."

Ben laughs in surprise as Professor Washington leads all of us out onto the quad. "Did you buy it just for the class?"

I nod. "The class description said phone cameras were insufficient."

He shakes his head. "Why are you taking this class? You've got to be pretty far along in your degree."

"Yeah." I stare at the ground as we step back into the sunshine, trying not to feel like that was a backhanded comment about my age. "It seemed fun."

"I guess that's how I got into it originally." He smiles. "Well, how about this? I'll shoot first, give you a few pointers."

I open my mouth to agree then remember all the pictures of women in his portfolio that looked weirdly like me. Did he set this up to get more of those?

It doesn't matter. I can't back out now without looking as crazy as I probably am."

"Sure." I offer him the smile I practiced.

It seems to work. As the class spreads out across the quad, he leads me to a tree off to the side.

"Perfect." He nods. "Sit in front of the trunk. Can you put on your jacket?"

I jump. How does he know I stuffed a jacket in my backpack, just in case the temperature dropped? Then, I look at my bag and see the tip of the maroon sleeve jutting out of the zipper.

Just be normal, Marcie.

I pull the deep red suede moto jacket out, put it on, then zip it up at his request.

"Why?" I ask.

"Color contrast." He smiles. "The grass and leaves still on the tree are really green, the sky is crazy blue, but the bark is this nice brown that'll look great with the jacket." His lips turn down for a second then flatten back out. "Sorry, could you take your hair down? It'll complete the look."

I need a picture of him. I pull the elastic out of my messy bun, and my long, dark hair cascades around my shoulders.

"Awesome." He pulls out his camera and lies on the ground in front of me. "Better perspective down here. Can you just try to look natural? Like you're relaxing."

I can't imagine anything I'd be worse at. I lean my head against the tree—have to shower when I get home; I can feel bark catching my curls, and if I fall asleep with that in there I'll have a Ryan dream—and go for the same smile I practiced on the way over.

The camera flashes. My stomach flips.

"Why did you join this class?" I ask before I completely lose it.

"Grab two of the leaves and hold them up in front of your eyes. Think playful." Ben hums. "Are you asking about the class, or about photography in general?"

"Photography, I guess." I don't like not being able to see him, but I obey.

He makes a disappointed noise. I don't think I managed "playful."

"It's a long story." He purses his lips. "Can you put the leaves in the neck of your jacket? And tilt your face toward the sky. Think contemplative."

"I'll do that if you answer." I remove the leaves from my eyes happily.

He laughs. "All right, fine. I went to college undecided. Completely adrift. When I actually dragged myself to social events, I spent half the evening standing on the sidelines and watching. Which was actually pretty interesting. And say what you will about phone cameras, they're accessible. So, watching turned into documenting. Documenting turned into sharing with my friends, then half the school as word spread. I just think there's something really cool about capturing a moment and making it permanent." He smiles softly. "Like taking control of time."

I blink a few times. Ryan wanted to be a director because he wanted to tell stories, wanted to be the "outside" observer that made those stories something other people could see. *Totally different.*

Right?

"Leaves?" Ben says.

I stuff handfuls of them into the neck of my jacket. They froth around my face like a neck ruff. My skin itches, but I tip my face up to the sky.

"And another part of photography is admitting when you're wrong," Ben says ruefully. "You look like you're auditioning for a really avant-garde Shakespeare play."

My mouth falls open, and to my own surprise, laughter comes out. I pull a handful of leaves from my jacket and throw them at him.

The camera flashes. He looks at the viewfinder then back up at me. "Beautiful."

14

ROLE REVERSAL

MARCIE

"MY TURN," I blurt. There's something way too earnest in his blue eyes. It crawls over my skin, icy and strange.

Ben blinks. "Oh. Uh, yeah. You want to use your camera or mine?"

"Mine." I yank the rest of the leaves from my jacket, then shed it entirely. It's way too hot for a jacket anyway. I stuff it back in my bag then pull out my camera.

Compared to Ben's, it's dinky.

But he's a professional photographer. There's no point in comparing. I just need to get a good enough shot to convince myself I'm making things up.

"Uh, go sit," I say. "No, you did that. Stand."

"You can do stuff I did." Ben stands in front of the tree. "I am, in theory, the teacher."

Don't remind me. I set up a simple shot. He's tall enough that I can use his body to mark the thirds in the picture.

It looks terrible. I take it anyway. But when I look in the viewfinder, his eyes are closed.

"You blinked," I say.

"Sorry." He smiles awkwardly. "We can do one where I'm holding my eyes open?"

"I think Kubrick covered that," I reply.

Ben frowns. Another tick against the Ryan column. He saw everything Kubrick ever made, and he would've gotten my reference in a heartbeat.

"What if you lie down? On your back." I grimace. That'll look like a corpse. Ryan's funeral was closed casket, I heard, but I really don't need that visual. "I mean your side." I squat and ready myself.

Ben drapes himself over the grass. "Paint me like one of your—"

The camera flashes. I check the picture.

"Eyes closed again."

"Sorry again." He rubs the back of his head. "I'm not really used to being on this side of the camera."

Maybe if I get closer. I only really need his face. I squat-walk a little closer. "Shy?"

"Not really." He smiles at my approach. "Want anything new?"

"Uh…." What else? That one look at his portfolio really didn't tell me enough about posing. His arms look awkward, but I don't know what to do about that. "No. If not shy, then what?"

"You're going to laugh."

I take the picture, check it. "Eyes closed again. Laughing will be better than the crying I'm going to do if you don't stop—what, flinching?"

"Fine." He shakes his head and rolls onto his back like he's forgotten I'm taking pictures. "My mom is seriously protective, and that extends to people taking my picture."

My stomach plummets to my toes. I don't take another picture. I can only see him in profile anyway.

That sounds just like Ryan.

"Protective how?" My voice sounds strangled. I feel strangled.

He glances at me, then pillows his arms under his head. "Couple years back, my dad and I were in an… accident." He swallows. "He died. I didn't. Since then, she's been edgy."

He doesn't have both parents. Just his mom. Like Ryan.

My mouth charges ahead of my brain. "I had a friend like that once. His mom thought he was going to get kidnapped. No pictures—and definitely nothing online."

Ben laughs. "Fuck, that's crazy."

The word stings. I know better than to flinch. While he's distracted, I snap a picture, and he doesn't flinch either.

"Nah, Mom just… never really got over how close she was to losing both of us." He holds his hand up, studying the webs between his fingers. "So now, she feels like any connection to the outside world is another opportunity to lose me anyway, pictures included."

My chest aches. "That must've been lonely."

Ben flips onto his side again and shrugs. "I've never known anything else."

He definitely seems less upset than someone with that much loss in his life would be. If he and his dad were in the same accident, he might've been as close to his dad's death as I was to Ryan's. How is he so relaxed?

"You just said the accident was a couple years ago," I say.

A nervous chuckle escapes his lips. Sensing an opportunity for revenge, I snap a picture. When I look in the viewfinder, my chest aches again. The framing and composition are shit—I really don't have an eye for this—but there's something about it. He looks so care-free, his eyes catching the sunlight, his sharp jaw cradling the soft line of his mouth.

He's beautiful too. *Just like Ryan was.*

Professor Washington claps her hands. "All right, folks, I want at least three fully edited pictures on my desk Monday, though you can add more if you think more are good. Get out of here."

I realize my knees are aching slightly from being bent for too long. Ben and I moved away from the tree for brighter lighting a dozen shots ago, and I don't think I've moved my legs since then. He snaps a final picture—me, with my own camera to my eye—and turns to put his camera away. My cheeks ache from smiling. I can't keep losing track of how much time I'm spending with him. I feel like hours are disappearing.

"I have another class." My heart pounds in my throat as I shove my camera away and grab my bag. "Thanks for posing. Have a good—whatever."

Then, I hop to my feet and turn toward McKinley. I have half an hour until my lab, but he doesn't need to know that.

"I can walk you," he says.

"Really, I'm good." I don't look behind me, just start to race away.

"Hey."

The soft edge to his voice freezes me in my tracks. Is he… hurt? I glance over my shoulder.

Ben stands alone in the middle of the quad, his hands in his pockets. "I had a really good time last night. And today. Is that just me?"

After all his awkwardness, I didn't expect him to be so direct.

"No," I say, too startled to lie.

"Okay." He takes a step closer, smiling. "Then is the class thing what's making it weird? Because I can be professional."

I shake my head. That should be the end of things. But he just keeps standing there, waiting, like he has nowhere else to be.

Dana's voice in my head: *Don't indulge.*

"You remind me of someone." I stare at Ben's shoulder. "Someone I don't really like to remember."

He exhales slowly. "Okay. Can I ask who?"

I shake my head. I barely recognize myself. Two days, two new people who know—at least a little—about Ryan. I can't say anything more.

"All right." He's quiet for several long seconds. If I couldn't see his shoulder, I'd think he left. "Well, how about this?" He steps closer and puts out a hand for me to hold. "Let me take you out again this weekend. Saturday night, if you're not busy. And I'll make sure you have the kind of night you couldn't possibly confuse with any other."

My brain screams. Dana's voice, Heather's, my own. Everything in me agrees I shouldn't do this.

But this close, I can see the bottom of his face in my peripheral vision. His mouth curls up in a smile so soft it can only be called fragile. Like a baby bird, just hopping out of the nest for the first time. I never saw Ryan—brash, confident Ryan—smile like that.

"Okay," I say.

15

OPENING A WINDOW

MARCIE

"I'M glad your schoolwork is going well." The next day, Dana takes a few notes and glances over her glasses at me. "But you know we're not just here to get you to graduation. How have things been socially?"

"I think I'm actually better friends with Heather." I smile. Ever since my Ben-Ryan confession, she's been really sweet. Waiting the extra five minutes before leaving for work so she can check in with me. Picking up snacks I like from Bean and Gone. Asking me to hang out. I've been kinda by myself for so long that I forgot what having real friends is like.

"That's wonderful." Dana smiles. "Do you know what precipitated the change?"

I stare at the geometric pattern on her carpet. After class yesterday, I broached the topic of Ben with Heather again. Not anything about the date, just... the idea of trying to be friends with him. Build up my tolerance–or whatever. Heather recoiled like I said I was going to try meth just to see what it was like and spun off on a huge speech about how, yes, exposure therapy is a thing that works sometimes, but it's overrepresented in popular culture, and you can only do it with the help of a therapist. I took that as a blinking neon sign that she isn't going to be thrilled about the date. And based on all my other sessions with Dana, I'll bet she'd feel the exact same way. Better to leave Ben out of the story entirely.

"Uh, no." I fiddle with the hem of my shirt. "Maybe because I went to her homecoming party?"

Dana nods. "You showed her you're someone who will accept invitations, so now you're receiving more of them. This is what I was talking about. Acting like the person you want to be."

She's been trying to get me to build up a social support network since I left the hospital. Maybe some of her advice really did help me with Heather.

Oh, God, how am I going to go on a date with just me to rely on?

"And I met someone," I say quickly. I'll just skip the details.

"Oh?" She takes a few notes. "Your last romantic entanglements were...."

"Disastrous." I nod. My virginity disappeared sometime in the partying phase that followed my arrival on campus. When I try to remember who has it, I end up with a parade of guys with too many Ys in their names—Bryden, Kaylen, Dylyn—and a generic, handsome-ish face. I've just decided not to worry about it. "But those weren't really romantic. They were physical. I was—how did you put it?"

"Using them to fill the hole in your life," Dana replies wryly.

I laugh, and she shakes her head. The first time she said that, back when I was still in inpatient, I laughed for the first time in months. She refused to see the innuendo for weeks after the fact, and now only acknowledges it when I force her to.

"Exactly." I smile. "But... I haven't really liked anyone since, you know, Ryan."

Saying that feels like an insult to his memory. I didn't just like him. I was head-over-heels in love with him, like a high school movie cliché.

"Then I think this is good." Dana runs her fingers through her red hair. "Because Ryan is…?"

"Dead," I mumble. At least I don't taste his blood every time I say that out loud anymore. I don't even know if any blood got in my mouth that day. It seems impossible, and yet…

Dana sets her pen down and meets my gaze. "You know I don't make you do that to be cruel, right?"

"I know." I sigh. "It's to make me face my grief and accept it."

"I think that's become just another mantra to you." She shakes her head. "I want you to hear me, Marcie. Ryan is dead, and you are alive. So your responsibility is to let each of you be what you are. Enjoy this new guy without thinking about him."

I nod, trying to hear her, but she's given me this speech so many times. My mind drifts away.

And it lands squarely on the matter of pictures. I've got the ones of Ben on my laptop now, saved both in an obvious folder for the class and one I labeled "Emails from Professors." But I don't have anything of Ryan to compare them to. The pictures I had are just gone, no sign of them even in the trash I looked up how to find on a phone.

"Are you listening to me?" Dana says.

I nod. "I'm hearing you. Acceptance. Living my life. He would want me to be happy."

"Good." She smiles. "That is our session time for today, but I'll see you Friday?"

I agree, grab my bag, and walk out.

It's not like I don't know Ryan's dead. Of course, he is. I watched it happen. If I didn't believe that, I would be going crazy again, and if the last time is anything to go by, someone would've noticed. So I can't be crazy. I just can't stop thinking about those missing pictures. As far as I can tell, nothing else was deleted. Nothing moved, nothing even edited. Just the pictures.

An awful thought floats through my mind. What if I was crazy, and now I'm not, and I hallucinated the pictures?

That's not possible. I shake my head as I step out of Dana's office building into the sun. It's a crazy thought, and I'm not having those.

Fuck, if I could just see one picture of Ryan and compare the two, I could stop fixating on this!

An idea begins to take root. I've spent days going through my phone now, running down every possible place a file could be hiding. I'm more familiar than ever with what I have on there. And something I have—despite the fact I've never felt compelled to use them in six years—is all the contacts from the phone I used in high school.

I turn the corner away from Dana's building then sit down on a bench and pull out my phone. This is definitely indulging. But I said in session that I like Ben, and I'm actually starting to think that might be true, and if there's a way to date someone I like without my insane fixations ruining everything, I have to take it. I open my contacts and begin scrolling.

Dozens of names slide past, each with their own stories attached. Megan Spencer, the prom queen. Jamie BIOLOGY, who I only worked with for one project and who shot milk out of his nose in the lunchroom. Beth with three hearts after her name, who I completely forgot I used to volunteer with at the soup kitchen one weekend a month. When I changed my name, I changed my number, but I kept the contacts because I wanted to know if anyone found me. That didn't seem sad until now.

Finally, I land on the name I am looking for. Theresa Simpson. God, I got her phone number before I even really started using emojis. It's weird to see it sitting there, unadorned, when once upon a time she was one of the two most important people in my life.

I haven't seen her since the day before Ryan's funeral. I haven't even wanted to reach out to her in the six years since then.

This isn't really reaching out. It's just peace of mind. Dialing one number won't bring the whole town down on me.

Before I can chicken out, I hit the "call" button. The line rings, and rings, and rings. I tap my feet, stare at the sky. Just when I decide this was stupid and I'm going to hang up, it connects.

"Hi," I say breathlessly. "It's Mar—Lily."

16

OLD FRIENDS

Marcie

"Lily," Theresa says. "Lily Nelson?

My other best friend from high school sounds exactly the same as I remember and nothing like herself. The helium-inspired bubbliness is gone from her voice, but my name rolls off her tongue just like it used to.

On the other side of the cafeteria, the jocks roar with laughter. Theresa rolls her eyes.

"Do they think we'll forget about them if we look away for too long?" she asks.

I shake my head. "I think it's like a mating call. Lions roaring in the jungle."

Ryan laughs. "There are no lions in the jungle, Li—"

I suck in a deep breath and clutch the splintery edge of the bench I'm sitting on. Warm September sunlight surrounds me, warm like it never would have been in Indiana at this time of year. I'm at college. It's been six years. I'm here.

"Yeah." My voice breaks. "It's been a while."

"It certainly has." She sounds a little stiff. "What, six years? A little more?"

"Six years, three months, and eighteen days," I rattle off automatically. Shit, I wasn't supposed to be tracking the days since his death anymore. "Uh, sixteen days, I guess." I last saw Theresa the day before Ryan's funeral.

Splintery bench. September sun. I'm here.

"Right," she says.

Silence hangs between us. The question about pictures, any proof of Ryan, pounds at my lips, but I know it's going to sound crazy. Maybe I can offset it by being very, very normal first.

"So, how are things?" I ask as casually as I can manage.

Theresa coughs a laugh. "Since six years ago? A lot has changed."

"That… makes sense." I pick at one of the nails on my free hand. "You went to Franklin, right?"

"Mm-hmm," she says.

More silence. Something is wrong, but with my heart hammering in my ears, I don't know what. We used to be able to talk for hours without stopping to breathe, it felt like.

"Did you end up getting your teaching degree?"

"Yeah, a couple years ago now." She sighs. "Middle childhood education, so I ended up back at South Dearborn Middle."

"Very cool." I tug on a hangnail, and it starts to bleed. "So, do you teach a specific subject, or…?"

"Social studies, for seventh and eighth grade."

Somewhere past the phone, someone starts crying. My heart leaps into my throat.

"Uh, do you—"

"Shit, yeah, hold on." The unmistakable rustle of a phone set on something soft scrapes through the speakers.

In the distance, I hear low murmurs. Comforting. Tears prick at the corners of my eyes, and I stick the hangnail in my mouth just to pull on it harder. September sun. Nothing to worry about.

The phone rasps back up. "Sorry, Teddy woke up from his nap early. Do—"

"Teddy?" I ask, barely hearing the start of her question. "Is that, uh… I mean, do you have kids already?"

"What do you mean already?" She offers a strained laugh. "I don't think I've done anything but grade papers and go to baby showers since I graduated from college."

"Of course." Theresa doesn't know I'm still in college. She didn't mean that as a backhanded compliment. "How old is he? Are you, you know, married?"

Another strained laugh. "Teddy's going on two next month, and yes, Jackson and I tied the knot well before I got pregnant, *Mom*." She clears her throat. "We've got a second on the way already, a little girl I'm going to name Dahlia."

My head swims. Teddy, or Theodore, and Dahlia were the baby names she picked out when we were ten. I can still remember her scribbling them on construction paper, her perfect little family. She dated Jackson Shields our senior year. She went to prom with him. She was inside with him when—

"I asked, did you call for a reason?" Theresa's voice is tight.

Pieces snap into place. My face burns. When Ryan died, I couldn't face anyone. I answered Theresa's texts sporadically that last summer, avoided the pool I knew she was working at. I barely left the house, so that was easy. When I smashed my phone, I didn't give her my new number. I don't even think I told her I was getting institutionalized. In that memory of Theresa drawing her perfect family, Ryan lies next to her, drawing himself with about a thousand dogs, all named Lightning. The three of us were inseparable after he moved to town in first grade. She lost both of her best friends in one night.

And I never said I was sorry. Fuck, I barely remember what I said to her the last time I saw her.

The bench, the path, the trees around me all start to go wavy. My breath speeds and slows. I can't feel my body anymore. All of this is signs of a massive flashback, the kind that leaves me shaking for hours if not days.

My gaze snags on my backpack at my feet. I have a lab report for Integrated Human Anatomy due tomorrow, and we did the lab in class, but I haven't even started collating my notes yet. Bile claws at my throat, but I swallow down the apology and the memories with it.

As sanely as I can, I say, "Uh, yeah. I was thinking about the old days and wondering if you had any pictures of Ryan because I seem to… not. Anymore."

Theresa snorts. "I've got pictures, videos, and the whole box of crap you dumped on me the day before the funeral."

Oh, God, I'm a monster. She doesn't even need to know I'm crazy to hate me. And I can't apologize without thinking about that day.

"Great!" My voice squeaks. "Could you maybe email me the pictures?"

She sighs. "Yeah, Lil. I'm at the start of the semester, and Dahlia's already keeping me up at night, so it might be a little while though."

I nod like she can see me. "Absolutely. No problem. Take all the time you need with Dahlia and Teddy and Jackson and everything else."

"I need an email address," she says quietly.

"Right." I only have one. Reluctantly, I rattle off my school email, with my new name.

"Huh," she says. "I guess you really did leave everyone from Dillsboro behind."

"I—" Wavy trees, wavy me. "I'll call again soon. At a better time. So we can really talk. Okaythanksbye!"

I hang up the phone, but just before the call cuts off, I hear Theresa's disbelieving laughter.

17

UNFORGETTABLE

MARCIE

FOR REAL, I text Ben, *I need to know where we're going so I can get dressed.*

With the message sent, I return to pacing back and forth in my room. I'm going to wear a track in the carpet, but it's 5:15, half an hour before Ben's supposed to pick me up for our second date, and he still won't tell me where we're going. I told him to pick me up because hiding where I live from him was crazy, and I'm not crazy.

Tell that to the billion and a half outfits I've considered and discarded, now covering my bed.

My phone vibrates, and I nearly break a nail opening it, desperate for it to be the email from Theresa that still hasn't arrived.

Just a response from Ben. *Close-toed shoes. And (as much as I hate to say it) probably not a skirt or dress. Embrace not knowing!!*

Apparently, the surprise is part of what will make this date so special. Maybe I have enough to get dressed, at least.

He texts that he's here as I'm finishing my braid. I race into the living room. Heather and Everett are curled up on the couch, "watching" some movie.

85

"Bye!" I call.

"Text me!" Heather yells back. "As often as you need to. Like, every hour."

"I'm going to be fine." I grab my keys. At least the overall shorts I settled on have enough pockets that I don't need a bag.

"I'm serious." She twists to look at me. "I don't think this is a good idea, and I want to make sure you're safe."

I never even told her I was going out with Ben. I just told her I was going out. I wave and bolt through the door. Down the stairs, around the building, and to the little cul-de-sac where Ben is hopefully still waiting.

He leans out of the window of an indistinctly brown sedan. "Hey! I thought Morgengraun might've gotten you."

I laugh and slide into the passenger seat. His car has total grandma vibes, from the ancient cloth seats to a bleached spot on the dashboard where I imagine a Jesus statue used to sit, but it's clean, and the air freshener hanging from the rearview mirror isn't overwhelming or shaped like a tree.

"You ready for an unforgettable night?" he asks.

I buckle in. "I guess we're about to find out."

He chuckles and pulls away from the building. A quick glance out of the corner of my eye tells me he followed his own dress code. He's got on a navy T-shirt with a couple brighter blue stripes across the chest that bring out his eyes, a pair of loose cargo shorts, and some beat-up sneakers. Cute-casual. And we definitely look like we're going to the same place, which is a great sign. I relax as he turns up the music.

"Oh, come on," I say. "Tell me you don't like soft rock."

"Sometimes it's good!"

The drive passes quickly as we argue about music. I don't have as many favorite bands as I do least favorite, and Ben considers himself a "musical omnivore," so he finds my taste snobbish. We laugh the whole way, our barbs harmless and playful.

"All right, after this next corner, you should be able to figure it out," he says finally.

I sit up in my seat, peering through the windshield as we turn. A squat, gray building with a neon sign reading "Tony and Toni's Laser Game Emporium" comes into view, and my stomach drops.

Laser tag was one of Ryan's favorite hobbies. He called it paintball's superior cousin. Half the pain, twice the fun. Every birthday, the three of us—and however many other friends he could convince his mom to invite—trooped out to the one sad little laser tag place near town and played until either our stomachs hurt from laughing or our legs hurt from running.

"Well?" Ben asks.

Is this a sign? Is he really Ryan, and he's trying to see if I know?

"Uh...."

"Ah, fuck." He grimaces. "You hate go-karts, don't you?"

I blink. "What?"

He pulls into the parking lot, parks, then gestures through the window at a go-kart track I didn't even notice. "I'm sorry, they're a guilty pleasure of mine, but I should've figured they wouldn't make a great surprise. It's okay, we can just—"

I put my hand on his arm. Both of us freeze. Slowly, I withdraw it.

"Go-karts are fine." I smile sheepishly. "I'm not much of a laser tag person."

He laughs. "No worries. Me neither. Way over-hyped. But the karts?" His eyes sparkle. "I'm gonna make you a believer tonight."

I take a deep breath and let him lead me out of the car. I'm not crazy, and I'm not ruining this. I'm here to have fun. Humid, late summer air blankets me, and I'm immediately grateful I opted for the short-sleeved shirt. The sounds of the go-karts are inescapable as we approach. Screeching metal, loud pop music, and laughter blend into one overpowering wall of sound.

Ben bounces up and down like a kid as we wait in line, and his hair flops into his eyes. I laugh—Ryan never let his hair get that long —and he shakes more down until he looks properly emo. I flip my braid over my forehead and fan out the hair past the ponytail holder to mock him. By the time we reach the front, I've basically forgotten the laser tag behind us.

"Together or separate?" a bored teenager asks.

Ben looks at me.

"Um." I've never actually ridden in one of these before. "Separate."

Ben's smile flickers a little.

"To start," I add, not certain it's a promise I want to keep.

The teenager couldn't possibly care less. He just takes two of the roll of tickets Ben produces and ushers us onto the course. I slot myself into a bright orange kart, and Ben takes the green one behind me.

"It's just like driving," he calls forward. "Except there's a winner."

A long-dormant competitive spark ignites in me. "Oh yeah? Is that why you wanted to ride together? To go easy on me?"

He laughs. "Don't worry, I have no intention to go easy."

The rest of the karts fill as we trade easy smack talk. Then, the teenager flicks on a mock stoplight. Red, then yellow, then green. I slam on the gas.

Ben shoots out ahead, and I yell. The kart's engine vibrates through my skin, up into my bones. I can't think about anything but the crappy controls, the pounding bass of the music, and the lime-green kart in front of me. One lap passes, then two. On the third, I cut past him at one of the corners and flip him off. The moment of celebration costs me, though, because he slides past me on the outer wall like he's a goddamn professional driver and hits the finish line first anyway. The rattling engines die, and the karts drift to a stop.

I stand and face him. "Again. You cheated."

He grins. "Prove it."

We race again and again. The sun sets overhead. I knock my kart into Ben's, sending him juddering softly into a stack of tires to claim my only win of the evening. The parents and children depart, leaving us with college students and teenagers who have nothing better to do. The track turns vicious, and I spend a whole race trying to coax my stupid kart back forward after a pink kart knocks me a full 180.

After that, I march up to Ben and stick out a hand to shake. "Truce. We need to take that pink-haired bitch down."

He glances around until he spots the teenager with hot-pink streaks in her hair. "Truce. You want to ride together?"

My body warms. "Okay. But after this, I think my old bones can't take anymore."

"Then let's go out with a bang." He grins.

Something flutters in my chest. I nod.

When the next race starts, we take a bright-red two-person cart. Ben assigns me the pedals, so I assign him the wheel. His body is hot against my back, and I force myself to focus. That teenager is going to regret the day she messed with me.

The two-person kart is slower, but it has a lot more ramming power. Ben and I move together like a wrecking ball. I switch between gas and brakes at his call, just barely audible over the noise. Competitors fall left and right as we gain on the pink kart. Just... a little... closer....

Wham! We make contact, and she spins directly into the tires. From there, we only need to coast over the finish line while the rest of the contestants fight with their karts.

I cheer and start to leap out of the faux leather seat, but Ben holds on. I look up into his blue eyes, and for the first time, I'm not thinking about anybody else.

He kisses me.

1 8

TO THE WIND

MY RIBS START to crush my lungs. I open my mouth in shock. He presses forward, and I can't help it. I flinch back.

Ben releases me immediately. "Sorry, I didn't mean.... Well, I guess—"

"It's fine." I unfasten the belt holding me in the kart and climb out. "Really."

"O...kay." He follows me slowly. "I can take you home now. We don't have to do the rest of the date."

My heart thunders. Heather's warning about being safe rings in my ears. I shake my head.

"What 'rest' is there?"

Awkwardly, Ben leads me into the Laser Game Emporium proper. It's even louder in here, the laser tag warring with the arcade. The smell of fried food winds through the air, and he gestures to a smorgasbord of options that make my mouth fall open again. I've never seen so many food choices in one place.

"I figured we'd pick a selection, and then, uh, I have a picnic

91

blanket in the trunk, and they close the track in half an hour." He shrugs. "Thought we could eat under the stars."

I am having a good time, so I take his hand. The slide of someone else's fingers against my own is strange, and I realize abruptly how little I've touched people since I was institutionalized. He has calluses on his fingers that make me wonder where they came from since he's a photographer, after all.

He smiles softly. "Okay. Let's do it."

After the go-karts, I'm starving, so we leave the building absolutely laden down with food. Things I've been eating since forever, like chicken fingers and french fries, as well as things I've never heard of before, like fried candy bars. The "picnic blanket" turns out to be pretty obviously his comforter from his college twin bed, but that doesn't stop me from smiling as he treks up a small hill overlooking the track. It's quieter than I thought it would be, and when they shut down the go-karts, the stars shimmer.

I am having a good time, so I pull out every trick for a good date that I've ever known or read about or seen in a movie. I gorge myself on the food like I'm not self-conscious, trying a bite of everything and reviewing everything in silly voices. When he starts to relax a little, I begin a contest over who can catch more fried marshmallows in their mouth. When he kicks off his shoes, I do the same and twine my ankles with his. That's so much less intense than the kiss, but it hums through me all the same. His leg hair scratches my ankles. I tell every funny story I've ever known, laugh at his jokes, toss my hair over my shoulder and bat my eyes. I made it weird, so it's my job to make it normal again.

After a while, Ben lies back against the blanket and points at the sky. "That's Orion."

I join him, follow the line of his finger. "That bright one there?"

"Mm-hmm!" He smiles. "Or it's the center of his belt, at least."

This is a classic romantic moment. I just wish I knew any constellations. "Where's the rest of him?"

"There?" Ben points.

It just looks like a bunch of dots. "Point more? I don't see it."

"Okay, I know way less about stars than I should." He drops his hand with a laugh. "Actually, pretty much just the middle-of-the-belt one. Used to know more." His voice grows thoughtful.

If I'm not allowed to drift away, neither is he. I roll up onto my side and look down at him. The stars sparkle in his eyes, and my gaze drifts down to his mouth. It would be so easy to kiss him. A normal girl would.

He cannot be Ryan, Dana's voice in my head reminds me.

Be safe, Heather's urges.

Call me when you can, baby. Mom's voice, with a crackle of static like a half-remembered voicemail.

Eh, I think romances are cheesy. Ryan's, from I don't even know when.

I don't need to listen to them. I'm not crazy anymore. This time, I toss caution to the wind and kiss Ben.

He jerks like he's been electrified. For a second, I think I'm doing it wrong. I didn't really have a boyfriend in high school, the last time I was sane, and vodka-drenched memories don't exactly give me a great idea of technique. Then, delicately, he puts his hand on my hip. He's testing again, making sure I know I can leave.

And he still tastes like cinnamon, though that may be more due to the churro we shared than anything else.

Want floods me like it hasn't in a long time. Not cutesy crush stuff but actual desire. I lick along the seam of his lips, what I assume was the universal signal for "open up," but he keeps kissing me normally. His hand on my hip scoots a little higher, and his thumb hits a patch of my side laid bare by my shirt shifting. He freezes, and his fingers tighten.

I smile. He's lived with his mom all his life. He's inexperienced.

Which is really, really cute.

He pulls back. "What?"

"It's not time to talk." I rock back, then roll forward, straddling him.

Ben makes a soft, punched-out sound and grabs both my hips. His thumbs massage circles into my ribcage. I claim his mouth again. He opens under me and thrusts his tongue up into my mouth. He might not be the most experienced, but he's not just going to lie back and let me run the show either. Hot want courses through my veins, and I roll my hips against him.

He's already stiffening beneath me.

I groan around his tongue, thankful for the night and the distance from the track. No one is going to see us. Not that I plan to have sex with him. Unless that seems more like what a normal girl would do.

Focus, Marcie!

I grab one of his hands and coax it up until he's cupping my breast. He runs a tentative thumb over the surface, as if trying to find my nipples through overalls, a shirt, and a bra. I smile again and thread my hand into his hair.

His scalp is… textured. Pebbly, almost. I run my finger over the skin, trying to make sense of it. A nasty bout of acne? Eczema? My thumb catches the edge of a fine, straight line.

They're scars. His whole head is covered in scars.

I clutch my gauzy, powder pink skirt in trembling fingers, caught some-where between rage and despair.

"Fine!" Ryan shouts. "Think I'm making a mistake all you want, Lil. But I'm not going to miss my goddamn—"

A bright, brilliant light looms around the turn, and I freeze.

I freeze. Ben kisses me a second longer, then pulls back.

"Marcie?" he asks.

I suck in a shuddering breath. "I'm fine."

My ribs threaten to puncture my lungs. I haven't flashed back to that moment in years. Only iron willpower keeps me from falling apart.

"Okay," he says. "But I think I'm done."

I nod and climb off his lap. Crickets fill the awkward silence.

"How did you get the scars?" I blurt.

His shoulders tense. "Long story. I didn't realize how late it was. We should go."

I nod robotically. Super normal, Marcie. Great job. We clean up the remains of our feast in silence. In the car, Ben turns on a country station, the only genre we both agreed we didn't like.

If Ryan lived, he'd have scars like that. All across his head. Maybe down his neck and shoulders, but it's not like I've really seen Ben's neck and shoulders. Oh, God, is that why he grew out his hair? To hide them? Ryan never liked his hair long.

Suddenly, Ben stops in front of my apartment. I jerk against the seatbelt.

"Good night." He takes one hand off the wheel like he's going to touch me, then puts it back. "Hope you had a good time."

I nod again. If I open my mouth, I won't be able to hold back the torrent of questions. Ben said he was in an accident, but not what kind. Was he in a hit-and-run? Did an SUV splatter his skull in the middle of a fight with his best friend?

Could I possibly be right?

I climb out of the car and begin the suddenly long walk to the apartment. The shadows seem long and hungry. I turn the corner to the metal stairs that will take me to my door. My phone vibrates, and I check the notification, expecting something from Ryan. *Ben.*

It's an email. From t.shields@sdearbornmiddle.org.

Theresa sent the pictures.

19

CRAZY

Marcie

I OPEN the email with shaking fingers. The body is nearly empty, just one line of inscription in the middle: *All I could find. Sorry.* But I don't care about that. Every molecule of my body narrows in on the attachment at the bottom. I click, and the picture fills my screen.

She obviously took this from under a table. No, a desk. I recognize the speckled, tan plastic that covers the bottom third of the image. Ryan leans close to the phone she was probably using during class with a goofy smile, his blue eyes crossed. It's a strange, slightly blurry picture.

And I don't care about that either because I was fucking right.

I don't need to open the picture I took of Ben after the night I spent with him. I'm not crazy. The two of them look identical. Same sandy blond hair with a few darker streaks. Same soft blue eyes. Same big ears, though they fit Ben's grown-up face better than Ryan's teenaged one. Same everything.

My stomach riots. My heart joins it, bouncing off my quickly collapsing rib cage. My breath races, and I realize I have one opportunity to outrun it. I wheel around and sprint up the stairs. It takes me three tries to get my key into the lock. The rattling scrapes around my skull, colliding with my spinning thoughts.

They look the same. I'm not crazy. Or am I? Does this mean I'm crazier than I've ever feared? This doesn't make any goddamn sense. I watched him die!

The door opens, and I fling myself inside the darkened apartment.

Heather yelps. Her outline against the glowing TV leaps closer to Everett. He clears his throat, clearly trying to seem too manly to yell. I scared them.

Good. I'm fucking scared.

"Marcie?" Heather asks.

I don't know. I haven't felt this much like Lily in a long time.

Someone turns on the lights. I stand in the open doorway, shaking. What if Ryan survived? What if he survived, and he's furious with me for abandoning him, for basically chasing him into the path of the car, and he's back to take his revenge?

Heather crosses the room to me. "What happened?"

My teeth chatter like I'm freezing. What if I never actually left the institution? What if I dreamed the last five years, and reality is finally forcing itself on me again?

She shuts the door, puts a soft hand on my shoulder. I jump. She doesn't know.

Or maybe she does. What if Heather hated me this whole time, and she found out about Ryan from someone else, and she hired Ben to make me seem crazy again so I'd get sent back to the institution, and she could have the apartment to herself?

Oh, God, I'm fucking crazy. And I can't get my mouth to work. I just shove the phone at Heather, still open to Ryan's picture.

"O…kay?" she says. "I don't—"

Everett hops over the back of the couch. "Seems to me all the whys don't make a difference until we get you chilled out a little."

I have never been hotter. I'm burning alive. Why am I trembling?

"Yeah, fuck." Heather shakes her head.

I expect the laughter to start—maybe they're both in on it—but instead, Heather kneels in front of me. Everett pauses the movie and heads into the kitchen. She starts untying my shoes, and the distinctive *hiss* of the kettle starting up reaches my ears.

They're… taking care of me?

Heather slips off my sneakers one by one. "How are your clothes? Comfy enough to hang out in?"

I couldn't feel my body if I wanted to. I nod automatically. One shred of control over myself has returned, I guess.

"She have a favorite snack, babe?" Everett calls over the breakfast bar.

"Those jalapeño chips in the top cabinet," Heather answers before I can wonder if she knows.

She's right. Technically. For this time of year. When did she learn that?

"Come on." She reaches for my hand slowly, giving me time to flinch.

Just like—

No, no, no. I force myself to take her hand. My arm swings like it's made of wood, and she doesn't even follow the progress with her eyes. Her hand is cool, smooth. Like the pale blonde ponytail that bounces against her back as she leads me to the couch. Nothing like the warmth of Ben/Ryan's hair.

She nudges me to sit, then drapes the thick, rainbow-colored quilt her grandma knit her last year over my lap. My trembling starts to slow. I can loosen my aching grip on my phone—not enough to drop it, in case the picture disappears like the others—just enough that my fingers stop hurting.

Everett pads over with a steaming mug of tea, a little bowl for the teabag, and the chips. I grab the chips before he's even finished setting the tea on the table and cram a fistful into my mouth. I used to hate spicy food. Dana taught me how it could be a grounding tool sometimes. People don't really taste in dreams. I don't taste my hallucinations.

My mouth prickles with heat, and I exhale through my nose. I'm not hallucinating everything. Everett drops onto the couch next to me, but a few respectful inches away. Heather sits on my other side.

"Okay," she says. "You want to relax for a minute? We can put the movie back on."

I shake my head. I need to show them the pictures, need to know if they see what I see. Fumblingly, I lift my phone and open it to the picture of Ryan again.

"Yeah," Heather says. "I saw that. What—"

"It's Ryan," I blurt. "Ryan. In senior year. If you look at the bulletin board, you can see a map, so I think it's Mr. Chung's AP History class."

"Who's Ryan?" Everett asks.

Tears bead in the corners of my eyes. It's been so long since I've heard anyone other than Dana say his name. Heather shakes her head at him, a silent "not now," and my chest aches with gratitude. I can't explain again, not at the moment. So I swipe to the picture of Ben I saved to my camera roll in case Theresa emailed me while I didn't have my laptop.

"Do you see?" I point at the hair, the eyes, the ears, switching back and forth between the two pictures. "They both have one dimple, too."

Silence falls. I look up to try to read their expressions and find them exchanging a look with one another. A *sorry, she's crazy* look. My heart hammers.

"No, you're not looking close enough." I zoom in on the picture of Ryan. "You see how his top left incisor is kind of twisted? He knocked it out of position when Tyler Maynard dared him to eat a rock." I switch to the picture of Ben. Fuck, the angle sucks. "I'm pretty sure you can see the same thing here—"

Heather bends over the phone and rubs my shoulder. "You know, I think you're totally right."

The pressure in my chest lightens. "Really? Because I don't know if I'm just making that up."

She shakes her head. "No, I think there's a definite...crookedness."

Oh, thank God.

"Hey, baby, weren't you just telling me about advances in that facial recognition shit?" she asks.

"Huh?" Everett blinks. "Uh, yeah, I guess."

"Everett's a forensic science major, and he's, like, really good." Heather rubs circles on my shoulder in time with her slow breaths. "You could probably take these pictures and compare them, couldn't you, baby?"

It's like the clouds opening after a thunderstorm. A real, scientific answer. Proof. I nod.

He peers at my phone. "With Ben laughing, and the angle of the picture on Ryan—"

"It'll be a breeze!" Heather says brightly. "*Right*, baby?"

I look up at the towering hunk of muscle I've barely given a second thought to before tonight. He looks down at me.

"Yeah, I've got it," he says.

I load the picture into one message, give him my phone so he can enter his email. Proof. I'm going to have proof. Hitting send feels like dropping weights onto the mat—or what I imagine that would feel like, if I lifted weights.

Heather takes the bag out of my over-steeped tea and hands me the mug. "We're trading off between action movies and rom coms. Want in?"

2 0

SOMETHING MISSING

Ben

I sip my cooling coffee and sigh. Photography of any kind is a dream job, and Scott gives me a lot of good assignments, so I'm never going to turn him down. But man, it's hard not to feel like something isn't missing when I want to make art, and I'm stuck counting smiles on interchangeable group shots.

This is just my first job away from home. There will be more.

My head itches below my unseasonal beanie. I ignore it. It's not like I need another reminder of my disastrous date with Marcie two days ago. I already feel stupid enough.

When I finally pick the shot with the most smiles, I take another sip of my coffee to discover "cooling" has officially become "cold." Perfect timing, I guess. I'll go grab a new cup from Bean and Gone. I email the picture to the editors, stand, and head through the warren of folding-wall cubicles as students start to trickle in after class.

Honestly, I was surprised to get an offer from a college paper. At my school, only students worked on it. But apparently the *Arkly* is so good that the newspaper for Sycamore Hollow, the town around the

103

school, went out of print decades ago in favor of it. So, hiring professionals is well within their budget.

I turn a corner just as Marcie's bouncy, blonde roommate, Heather, steps in the front door.

Fuck.

I duck into the nearest open door—a storage closet that reeks of powdered ink—and shut myself in, praying she didn't see me. Heather probably knows everything about last night's train wreck. I can just picture her cackling over my fumbles. She's got a cackling face.

And I have no idea how I'm going to get out of here without seeming like a crazy person.

Mom's simple rules for seeming normal. If somebody says something I don't recognize like I'm supposed to know it, agree. Look it up later if I have to.

Not useful here.

Names are important. Remember someone's name, and they'll assume you're on top of things.

Definitely not going to get me out of this closet.

Smile often, unless no one else is. Keep your hands in your pockets, unless you have something to do with them. When you say something wrong, laugh like your mouth messed up, not anything else.

When in doubt, you have an important errand to run.

Bingo!

I grab a ream of paper off one of the shelves and resign myself to the half-burnt coffee in the break room instead of Bean and Gone. I'll survive. Then, like I belong exactly where I am, I open the door to the closet and stride out.

No sign of Heather. Thank God.

Just thinking about her reminds me of Marcie. I spent all week planning that date. I even had a bottle of champagne in the car, if things went in a champagne direction. All that effort, and she just—

I shake my head. I'm normal. I'm just replacing the copier's paper and grabbing some coffee. When I return to my desk, there's a sticky note on my monitor in Scott's jagged scrawl.

Meet me in my office when you have a minute.

Mom, as much as I love her, isn't big on praise, so talking to Scott is like a sugar high. I crumple up the note and head over.

Scott's door is slightly open, but I knock anyway. He looks up.

"Ben!" His warm smile lightens his grizzled face. "Come in."

I slide inside and take the seat across the desk from him. In a month and a half, I've spent enough time in here that it's already familiar. To be fair, there's not much to be familiar with. A framed copy of the first edition of the *Arkly* hangs on the wall. Books on journalism crowd the one low shelf. A filing cabinet squats in the corner. Scott's desk is bare except for a cup of pens I've never seen him touch, his computer, and whatever book he's reading. Today, it's *Spoken Russian for Modern Use*, and his bookmark is a lot further along than the last time I saw that one.

"Couple things," he says. "First, I saw your shot for the golf thing. Really impressive work."

"Really?" The golf thing was a new course being built outside of town. I spent ages trying to find a spot that would let me capture the construction dirt that covers most of the area, the one finished water trap in the middle, and the bell tower of Sycamore Hollow in the background. By the end, I got pissed off and just snapped a whatever shot of the dirt and the water.

Scott laughs. "Modest. I like that. Next, you're going to be telling me you don't think the picture you snagged of that thunderstorm rolling in is front-page material."

I grin. That one, he's right about.

"How'd you like another assignment?" he asks.

"Always good!" I reply.

He hands me another sticky note with a few scribbled details. "Title's going to be *Future of Science on Our Doorstep*. Cheesy, I know. It's a puff piece for the dean."

I look at the note, then up at him, a smile spreading across my face. "Are you giving me a human-interest shoot?"

"Why, is that an interest of yours?" He feigns confusion, then laughs. "Have at it, kid. Impress the dean, and you've got a ticket somewhere better than this Podunk town. I hear he's got connections in Chicago."

"Yes, sir." I jump out of my seat, barely hearing him. Human interest means candids, which means working for my shots and liking them when I'm done. I love human models.

After a quick detour to my desk for my camera bag—no sign of Heather, thankfully—I head out into the late afternoon sun. Instantly, my pullover is too warm. I keep dressing like I'm in Illinois. Adjusting is hard when I've never been anywhere else.

No, wait, Mom said we used to visit her family in Oklahoma for the holidays. Right. I've left Illinois before now.

I cut through the quad toward the McKinley building the note indicated. Apparently, that's where the future of science lives. I step into a square hallway paneled with oppressively dark wood. Even from here, I can see a glimpse of a bright white classroom through a window in one of the doors. My fingers itch. I couldn't have invented a better assignment for myself.

I move through the dark halls like a ghost. Sometimes, I enter the classrooms, take a few shots from the back or even sneak around the side to get a better angle. One course lets out, and students flood around me. A guy with red hair forgot to remove his goggles from the top of his head, which I barely catch through the crush. Great pictures pile up on my SD card. That thing in my chest that hums when I'm doing something I love threatens to drown out the snap of my camera.

I wander one of the back halls, checking out each classroom. A chem lab. An anatomy lab, thankfully unused. Gore grosses me out. A regular amphitheater, full of students. On the floor at the front, one of them practices some life-saving technique on a dummy. I raise my camera.

And realize the student is Marcie.

Her dark braid whips over her shoulder as she turns to another student and demands something. The second student offers her a set of paddles. She presses them to the chest of the dummy, which jumps, then pauses as if she's waiting for something. Her mouth is slightly open—I adjust the zoom on my camera—and a sheen of wetness paints her lower lip. I know what that lip tastes like. Black coffee or powdered sugar, depending on the day, and always a little bit like some flower I don't know.

I snap a picture just as she mouths a curse and turns back to the dummy. She discards the paddles and slams her hands down instead, compressing its rubbery ribs. I know this one! CPR.

My finger flies on the shutter. Marcie looks so beautiful. Fearless. Nothing like last night when she touched my head and flinched like I bit her. Or maybe I'm just coloring her reaction in my memory.

I lower the camera. Fuck, if she can be fearless, maybe I can too. I pull out my phone and type up a quick message.

Hey, I'm sorry about last night. I'm a little sensitive about my scars, and I forget that surprise isn't a bad thing. Can we meet up again soon? Maybe talk? I draw in a deep breath. *I can explain, if you want*

I hit send. In the room, the whole class cheers. She rescued the dummy.

If you gave me another chance, you'd be a real lifesaver, I add with a smile.

21

PROOF

Marcie

"Nice work," a girl whose name I don't know says after our Nursing of Older Adults. "I thought Dummy-nic was a goner."

I blink a few times before the pieces slide into place. The old rubber test dummy I've been using for at least four years now gets a new name every year, and this year, it's Dummy-nic. She's talking about my save in the bronchodilator-cardiomyopathy example.

"Thanks." I smile awkwardly.

She nods and wanders off. People don't usually talk to me after class, but I always feel like I'm doing it wrong.

Whatever. I pound down the stairs while pulling my phone out of my back pocket, hoping for an email from Everett with results. We watched movies until I passed out on the couch last night, and Heather told me this morning that he said it might take a couple of days, but "might" means it also might not.

Nothing from Everett. But I do have a text from Ben. I swipe it open and read the message.

I'd be a real lifesaver?

The girl who just complimented me bumps into my shoulder and mutters, "Sorry."

I stopped in the middle of the stairs. I have to keep going.

Abruptly, goosebumps coat my skin. I'd be a real lifesaver. Just like I was for Dummy-nic. The sentence is awkward, stilted like he was trying to fit the idea in. It barely even makes sense with the rest of the message. Unless he saw me in there.

My heart slams against my rib cage. I spin around, looking for him like he's going to be waving at me through a window. Nothing.

Inhale. He's not Ryan because… because….

There's no way to finish that sentence. He could be Ryan. And he wants me to know he was watching me. I expel my breath in a gust of air and rush out of the classroom. I have to get home.

Maybe I am crazy. I never really expected "crazy" to be the better option, but it is now. All those pictures in his portfolio that looked like me. The just-wrong backstory, like he was leaving clues. Hell, his job is just barely wrong too. What's the difference between a photographer and a director, really? He wants me to know all of this, wants me to figure it out, but why—

I slam face-first into someone's chest and stumble back, my head ringing. A cloud of cigarette odor surrounds me like the stranger gives it off defensively, but he catches my shoulders before I fall.

"Fuck, sorry," I mumble.

The stranger scoffs. That's so abruptly rude after catching me that it actually shakes me out of my spiral for a second, and I look up at them.

Him. A him I actually recognize, which is a surprise, because I'm halfway across the quad so I'm dealing with Ardent gen pop. Pale skin, though I think less pale than last time. Dark, shaggy hair. Out in the sun, his face looks like someone carved it with a hatchet, and without the stress of a party beating down on me, I notice the tapestry of tattoos covering both his arms.

"You again," I say.

He rolls his eyes and releases me.

"Now who's the cartoon character?" His voice holds a hint of an accent I can't place.

Then, he marches past me, a black spot on the bright campus. Very weird. But he's leaving. The phone burning a hole in my pocket reminds me I have other weird people to worry about who very much aren't going anywhere. And I'm exposed out here, accessible from all sides. I duck my head and begin hurrying home again.

Ben—or whoever he is—was stupid enough to text me. I check my phone again. Yep, the message is still there. That means I have proof. I can report him to someone, maybe get him fired or banned from campus.

If anybody would accept a text with some weird phrasing as proof. Who would I report him to? Campus security? The *Arkly*? And for what, having scars and looking like someone? The more I think about it, the more it sounds like a one-way trip back to the institution.

Honestly, I wouldn't even blame them. I sound crazy. But somewhere in my gut, I know I'm not. I just need to convince everyone else.

I squash the voice in the back of my head reminding me I was certain last time too and look for somewhere a little less exposed. The library, converted from the old Anglican church they used to have on campus, looms over the quad. I barely ever go there because I got all my textbooks online, but I know there's a section in what I think used to be a choir loft that only has one way in and out in addition to a view of the main floor. It's perfect.

Because I can't go home yet. Heather can't know I'm doing this.

I dart inside and head up to the choir loft, right where I remember it. The books are all in French, so I have no idea why I went up here the last time I did, but it wasn't to read.

A blurry memory floats back to me, gin-soaked, of these floorboards denting my knees. I guess that makes more sense.

Well, like last time, I get on the floor, but I put my back to the shelf and stare out over the converted chapel. I have one real chance at proof, if Everett is going to take too long. I call Theresa.

"Wow," she says. "I didn't really expect you to call again."

Just hearing her voice sets the carved wooden bars of the railing separating me from the main floor wobbling. Did I call her one night during my partying phase? Did she call me?

"Yeah," I say. "Sorry about that."

"Was the picture not good enough?" she asks flatly.

Her voice becomes Ben's, becomes Ryan's mom's, becomes Dana's. It was stupid to come up here. I didn't know a memory would be waiting for me, but my hold on time and place is slipping through my fingers.

Fuck it. I'm not making it out of here clean. I owe Theresa better.

"I'm so sorry I abandoned you," I sob into the phone.

The world twists like a kaleidoscope, spinning endlessly backward.

2 2

BLAST FROM THE PAST

My shoulders heave, and I feel like I'm about to puke, but no tears come out anymore. I don't have any left. I roll over on my bed and stare at the thin streams of warm afternoon sunlight squeezing in through the gaps in my blinds.

Two days ago, at this time, I was out of school early, sitting next to Theresa at her mom's hair salon, primping for prom. I was holding her hand and laughing. I was complaining about Michaela because Ryan—

The sobs take me again.

He wasn't supposed to… to… I can't even think it yet.

Someone knocks on my door. I ignore it. Either Mom will just come in, or it's someone else, and I don't want to see them anyway.

The door creaks open. "Hon?"

Mom. I don't turn over.

"Do you want some lunch?" she asks. "I got another round of condolence gifts, and there's a platter of deli meat in here. I could make you a nice sandwich."

When she dragged me away from the scene two days ago, I was still screaming. I couldn't stop. My own words echo in my head on a loop—*stop, let me go back, they're not listening, I saw him take a breath, stop, please*—but I haven't been able to say anything since. My throat is raw. There's nothing else to say. I saw him take a breath, but the call still came in from his mom in the dead of night, saying—

"Okay," Mom says. "I'll just leave these in here. Let me know if you change your mind. The meat is downstairs in the fridge."

Plastic crinkles, the door shuts, and I sit up automatically. Somehow, everyone knows I was there. Cheap flowers and gift baskets block out the secondhand playbills I tried to paper my room with last summer. Some of them are already wilting, and I think I like those ones best.

Robotically, I march to the newest stack and begin opening cards. A still hairspray-crunchy curl sticks to my cheek, and it's getting harder to read through the days-old mascara, but I'm learning.

Mrs. Milankovitch, AP Chem. Brianna Chu—fuck, do I even have any classes with her? Did he? Have we since middle school? Andy Prince, the only guy he could tolerate on his basketball team, sent a box of chocolates. Or, more likely, his mom did.

But those are the only names I recognize. For the rest, I have to pull out old yearbooks, match last names to pictures. A freshman on the chess team. A sophomore who moved to town so recently they missed picture day. My stomach threatens to crawl out of my throat as I read each "heartfelt" message. They didn't know him. They don't know me.

They mean well, the Ryan in my head says with a shrug. *Or maybe they had big, fat, secret crushes on me too.*

I turn back to the pile. The smile on his bloody face in my mind is not helping my nausea, or the dry sobs scraping out of my throat. Last one, a faded bouquet of wildflowers that looks vaguely… familiar? I open the card and read.

I don't know how to do this, but I'm so fucking sorry. I made his bouton-niere out of these flowers from my backyard. I'm sorry. – Michaela Tucker

My sobs abruptly shift into a guttural scream. All the stillness of my last two days burns off at once. I throw the flowers on the ground and crush them under my bare feet.

"He asked you because he felt stupid going alone!" I yell. "And Theresa asked me, as a joke, so Ryan said he needed his own date! You were just *there*! You weren't anyone to him!"

Not enough. I scrape the remains of the flowers off my rug, yank open the blinds, throw open the window, rip off the screen, and toss them out.

"Hon?" Mom calls.

I have to move faster. She's going to stop me. More flowers rain out the window. Ryan didn't give a fuck about any of these people. How dare they try to claim him now? The gift baskets go next, fake grass flying everywhere.

"Lily, I'm coming upstairs," she says.

The flowers stained my rug. It's pinkish on the dingy tan, but all I can see is the spot next to it, where Ryan accidentally sat on a bar of chocolate the whole time we were playing Monopoly and ground it into the fibers permanently. Abruptly, I picture him there, ten years old again, grinning through bright-red teeth. The back of his head explodes off again. Mom's footsteps on the stairs. I start rolling up the rug as fast as I can to chase him off. He disappears.

The doorbell rings, and I flinch.

"One minute," Mom yells.

I try to take a deep breath, but suddenly Ryan is spinning the central portion of the first-place science fair medal we won together in sixth grade. I yank it off the post of my bed and throw it next to the rug. He's in my closet, wearing the outfit I put him in for a spirit day last year, dress up as your favorite person. Everywhere I look in this room, he's there, bloodstained and laughing. I yank one of the clear plastic bins Mom has been stockpiling to move me to college and start throwing things in. The strip of pictures we snuck out of a beach day. The playbill for my favorite show that he got me a few birthdays back. My once pale pink prom dress, still in the plastic police evidence bag that they just gave it back to me in. Everything has to go, everything that he touched or loved or knew. He's haunting it all.

The door to my room opens, and I don't even look up.

"Hey, Lil!" Theresa grabs my shoulders.

I fight her grasp. There's still too much of him in here. He hid in my closet during hide-and-seek. He slept in my bed, back when we were young enough for sleepovers.

"Look at me!" Theresa snaps.

I've never heard her sound like that. I obey automatically. Her gray eyes, red-rimmed from crying, burn into mine.

"What are you doing?" she asks.

I laugh helplessly. "An exorcism."

There's no pity in her eyes. No fear. "He's everywhere, isn't he?"

I nod, and I feel like a shaken-up soda bottle, a baking soda volcano. "I have to get him out."

"I'll help you," she says.

Together, we whirl through my room, cramming things into the box. She convinces me I can't get rid of my bed or my dresser, tells me all the memories without him that belong there, starts to replace her ghost with his. Finally, the box is too full to take anymore.

"Okay." She exhales slowly. "Now, what do you say we eat something, get some fresh air, and just chill for a little? We could watch that pro shot you're always trying to play during movie night."

Movie night with the three of us. I shake my head furiously.

"Lil, you gotta let someone in," she says.

I know who I want. But I can't have him anymore.

"Just take the box and go." I stumble back to my bed.

"I'll see you at the funeral tomorrow," she says before she leaves.

I don't answer her. All my words are gone.

2 3

MENDING FENCES

"Hey, Lily! You gotta listen to me," Theresa says.

That doesn't make any sense. She left. And why is my face wet? I cried all my tears out days and days ago. Something harsh and fast echoes around my room. I run my hands through my hair—

And find it's braided, something I never had enough hair for. Had. Back in high school.

"Come on, Lily, breathe," Theresa says. "You're scaring me."

I crack one of my eyes open. Dark wood railing. Shelves behind me. Book titles in French. Dana's voice whispers in my ear, coaxing me through a simple grounding exercise.

Inhale. I'm in the library at Ardent.

Exhale. The movement of the railing in front of me is my own rocking.

Inhale. Theresa's voice is coming through the phone crushed between my shoulder and my ear.

Exhale. It's been six years since Ryan died.

"Good," Theresa says. "Breathe slowly."

I suck in another breath and run my hands over myself. I'm bigger than I was then. My clothes are different. I haven't spoken to Theresa since that day.

"I'm so sorry." My voice is shaky, wet.

"Hey, it's okay—"

"No!" I say sharply. "I abandoned you. Selfish. Stupid. Awful."

"You were going through a lot." Theresa's voice is softer than it was at any point in our last call, even when she was talking about her kids. "Still are, I guess."

I shake my head. "Hasn't been this bad in… years."

That's true. A full-on flashback is going to wipe me out for the rest of the day. I need electrolytes and a snack.

"Was it really?" she asks.

"What?"

"That bad." She exhales slowly. "For you."

I almost want to laugh. "They locked me up, T. Too crazy to live."

"Shit."

Things are quiet for a while. Just having her here, having everything out in the open, is weirdly steadying. My hands shake like a leaf in the wind, but they'll do that until I get my snack.

"I was a bad friend," I say finally.

"Yeah." She sighs. "But so was I. I knew you were losing it, but I didn't have myself together enough to be there for you."

"You lost him too," I reply.

"Yeah, tell the town that." She chuckles bitterly.

A vision of her life spreads out before me. Ryan died, so everybody cared about him. I was there, so everybody cared about me. And Theresa got shuffled off to the side, the third wheel who nobody paid attention to, whose grief no one saw.

"I'm sorry," I say.

And something knits back together between us. Theresa immediately jumps to smoothing emotions out of the conversation, but instead of demanding to know why I've called or giving me one-word answers, she launches into a story about her class, then Jackson taking care of Teddy, then Dahlia keeping her up at night, then another story, and another. Slowly, I volunteer a few stories of my own. My classes. Heather. A funny mix-up in Bean and Gone the other day. I even laugh.

A story about Heather winds around to Everett, and I remember why I put myself through this in the first place.

"You said you still have that box I gave you," I blurt.

Theresa is quiet for a long moment. "Yeah."

"Can I have it?" I ask. "I'll pay shipping."

Another moment passes. "Are you sure you want that, Lil? It seems like staying away from stuff about him is a way safer bet."

It absolutely is. But she's using a gentle, dealing-with-a-crazy-person voice now. And if I tell her about Ben and the text, she's only going to think I'm crazier. *Think, Marcie, think!*

"I want to bury it," I say. "On campus. My therapist feels it would be smart if I had somewhere to grieve him here. That's, uh, what the picture was about too. I'm finally ready to deal with the memories."

God, that sounds good. I'd believe me.

"I guess that makes sense," she says. "You did kind of disappear from Dillsboro after everything. But I thought that was how some people grieve."

I shake my head. "That's actually the first stage of grief–denial."

"Huh," Theresa says. "Then I guess Ryan's mom is in denial too."

"That makes sense." I pause. "Wait, why do you say that?"

"Oh, she left town a couple weeks after you did. Hasn't been back since." She swallows audibly. "I've been, uh, tending his grave instead."

New tears sheet down my face. "Lavender?"

She laughs. "What else?"

Ryan loved lavender. The scent, the flower, all of it, but he refused to admit it to anyone but us.

"I'll send you the box on one condition," she says.

I agree automatically, barely listening. Thinking about Ryan this much makes it impossible to forget what sent me here in the first place: that text from Ben and my proof. There has to be something in that box that'll show everyone I'm not crazy.

Or if I'm crazy, it's only because he made me that way.

"When you bury it, plant lavender," she says. "I can't plant in the graveyard, but he always preferred it growing."

"Of course." A broad smile splits my face. I sweep away the rest of my tears. She said yes!

"And we should talk again soon," Theresa says. "I really have missed you all these years. I've got friends at school, but it's not the same."

"Totally." I nod enthusiastically, climbing to my feet. "Whenever you want. Just email me a time. Or text me! You have my number."

"I do." She chuckles. "Kinda weird to say."

"Right?" I bounce up and down, still shaky and spent but now infused with a new energy. I have to get back to the apartment, do some research on forensics, figure out what I put in that box that Everett can use. I'm so close now. "So, I have to go."

"That makes sense." She laughs again. "Bye, Li—"

I hang up the phone before she finishes and bolt out of the library. There's so much to do!

24

A LOSS

BEN

I TWEAK the colors on a photograph and check my phone. Nothing. That's fine. I open my email and type out a quick response to a private portrait request—not right now, but maybe around Thanksgiving—then check my phone. Nothing. Great. I sip my coffee, swirl the latte around in my mouth to taste the tiny remaining flecks of cinnamon, and… check my phone.

Nothing!

Fuck it. I open the message thread with Marcie and read what I sent over again. Yup, it seems just as normal as it did nearly two full days ago. I can't believe it's already Wednesday. Half a week between the date and now, and she still hasn't answered. Even a perfectly normal guy would start assuming he was being ignored at this point.

High-pitched laughter floats over the cubicles, and I jerk my head up. Heather is finally here. If anyone knows what I did wrong, it's going to be her. I jump out of my chair and cut across the *Arkly* offices to her desk. She's in the process of setting down her backpack, and two of her friends are standing around talking, so obviously she's not too busy for a social concern.

"—And anyway, we're going to kick Bennett's ass, like we do every year," one of Heather's friends, Stephanie, says.

"She'll kill you if you jinx it." Danny flips long dreadlocks over his shoulder. "The boyfriend needs the rivalry game to live or whatever."

Heather shakes her head and laughs just as I stride up between her friends and clear my throat. She looks up at me, her mouth still open.

"Hi, Heather," I say. "I wanted to ask you a question about Marcie."

She snaps her mouth shut then looks at Steph and Danny. "I'll catch up with you guys."

They shuffle away. Something is up. All the brightness and humor drains out of Heather's face, and she crosses her arms.

"So, I texted her the other day," I say, "and she hasn't gotten back to me yet, and I was just wondering if you know why, or if she said anything, or whatever."

She snorts. "You're seriously asking me?"

"Uh… yeah?" I frown. Heather is Marcie's best friend as far as I can tell. There's no one else to ask.

"Don't you have Scott's asshole to lick?" She turns to her desk and boots up her laptop.

Something flares in my chest. I'm not letting Marcie slip through my fingers, not like this.

"Please." I swing around and get into Heather's line of sight again. "I won't bother you like this again."

"She hasn't texted you back?" Heather whips back to me with a scowl. "Good. I'm gonna tell you this once, and only because I think you're kinda sad: stay away from Marcie. You're not good for her. You're never going to be good for her. I'm glad she's not texting you back, and I bet she has a good reason for it, because fuck me, she was excited to go out with you. So just chalk it up as a loss and walk away."

My mouth falls open. I expected a lot of different things—mocking, laughter, that weird, coy "talk to her if you really want to know" thing girls do—but Heather seems seriously angry.

"Walk away from me, too," she mutters as she turns back to her laptop. "Articles actually take time to write, believe it or not."

I don't know what else to do. I just start walking away. Marcie doesn't have a good reason not to text me back. The end of the date was awkward, sure, and I feel like shit about it, but I apologized. I offered to explain. Why is Heather angry at me? Is Marcie?

"Ben!" Scott calls from the open door of his office.

Like a plastic bag in the wind, I float along, following the sound of his voice.

"I wanted to ask—uh. You all right, son?" Scott asks.

I drop into the chair across from him. "I think I just got dumped."

"Ah." Scott glances around, his heavy eyebrows furrowed.

Mom's basic rules for seeming normal number fifteen: work is work, personal is personal. I jump out of the chair.

"Sorry, you're my boss," I say.

Scott shakes his head. "No, sit. I know you're all alone out here." He shuts the door behind me then leans on the front of his desk. "It's been a while since I've done this, but I take it you liked this girl?"

He seems to earnestly want to help. And it's not like I can go to Mom with this. I sink back into the chair, feeling how I imagine a kid in the principal's office must feel.

"Yeah." I rub the back of my neck, feel the latticework of scars hidden just under my hair. "Maybe more than that, but we just went on our second date, and I'm worried I scared her off."

Scott twists his wedding ring back and forth around his finger. "I'm pulling on old instincts here—the wife and I never had time for kids—but I don't suppose you told her how much you liked her?"

I shake my head. "I didn't do anything wrong that I know of! We ended on an off note, but I apologized and offered to fix it as soon as I got my head on straight. And it was just awkward, not awful. I thought."

Every second of the date up to that point was basically perfect. I'll remember the way Marcie fit against my chest in that last race for the rest of my life. Her cheeks went pink in the wind, and even when I mistimed that first kiss, she went out of her way to make sure I knew she still wanted to be on the date with me. And her body....

"Well, I'd like to think I know you pretty well," Scott says. "Working with a man tells you a lot about him. You're passionate, dependable, you don't sweat the small stuff. You're a good kid." He claps me on the shoulder, a gesture that feels fatherly even though I don't remember Dad ever doing it. "She's not worth it if she doesn't see that."

"No, you don't understand." But how do I explain the bright, tight feeling in my chest every time I see Marcie? There's a reason I take pictures. Words aren't my thing.

"I think I do." Scott shakes his head. "There's all this pressure on young people to become someone and all before you even turn thirty. Every job has to be your career, every trip has to be the vacation of a lifetime." He smiles, a slightly awkward expression on his face. "Every girl has to be the girl of your dreams. But if she doesn't realize what a catch you are, she's missing out, okay? Her loss."

I know Scott means well, so I smile, but I can't shake the feeling that I can't let Marcie get away. I'm not taking this loss.

2 5

THE PACKAGE

MARCIE

I FIDGET with my phone in line at the basement mailroom of Delacruz-Webb. Maybe it wasn't smart to cut out of Ethical Health and Technology early, but Professor Shields was going over a paper we'd been assigned, like, a dozen times. And it's a Friday.

And the box Theresa promised to send is here.

The line moves forward. I show my student ID to the bored attendant then receive the massive package. It isn't wrapped, just taped. The same box I remember. I mutter my thanks and hurry out.

My heart races as I rush home. I unlock the apartment door and re-lock it behind me awkwardly, juggling the oversized package. I feel like it'll disappear if I put it down. The dark living room means Heather has work today, which means she won't be back until dinner, but I still go to my bedroom and shut that door behind me, too. If only I could install a lock on that without voiding our security deposit.

With a huge exhale, I set the box down in the middle of my room. It looks exactly like I remember it. Mom's bubbly handwriting declares it property of Lily Nelson. The spot for the room number is still blank because Theresa took it before I got my dorm assignment. The world is already going wavy around me.

No. I'm not giving in, not when I'm this close. I rush to the kitchen and grab a new bag of jalapeño chips and a glass of ice water. Hopefully, together, they'll be enough to keep me present.

I return to my bedroom and rip the cover off the box.

Inside, it's like I imagine an archaeological site. Layer after layer of my life, Ryan's life, sit atop one another, creating a chaotic picture I have to reconstruct. The ice water disappears quickly. I begin sorting things. First grade, his arrival in town, goes at one end of the timeline. Senior year goes at the other. I shove fistfuls of chips into my mouth. Twelve years has never looked so small. Could we really only have known each other for that long?

While unearthing a hideous dog he painted for me in eighth grade, I realize come my next birthday, I will have known Ryan for less than half of my life. That's when the tears start. But I'm holding onto this moment with my fingernails, just barely not falling through time.

When I pull out the fourth page of pun names for his first movie that we used to write in study hall, it hits me that none of this is going to help. I've got handwriting samples, but the websites I've been staying up late reading say handwriting analysis is basically pseudo-science. Ditto for the coffee cup he sculpted with a bite out of it. Dental records are great, but a bite mark isn't the same. I'm reaching the end of the box—and the end of my sanity—and I'm going to end up with nothing.

I dive into the box without looking, and my hand hits fabric. Scratchy, poofy fabric. Tulle. My stomach flips, but I slowly withdraw my prom dress, the end of it just poking out of the police evidence bag.

More chips. I need more chips. I shovel them into my mouth, but I've grown used to the burn. A flashback threatens, a big one, and I'm terrified I know what it is.

I drop the dress and sprint into the kitchen. A bottle of cayenne pepper sits on the counter. I shake a mouthful onto my tongue and hold them there.

A forest fire rages in my mouth. I grab the counter and hold on for a long moment. I'm here. I'm in college. I need to face the dress if I want my answers.

Only when my nose runs do I pour myself another glass of ice water and wash out the spices. I'm steady. I slip the bottle of cayenne into my pocket and return to my room.

The dress, hem still spattered with Ryan's blood, stares back at me. I can do this. I'm not crazy. I kneel in front of the dress I wore on the worst day of my life and pull off the plastic covering.

Plink.

Something small and hard falls unmistakably to the wooden floor between my bed and the edge of my rug. I peer at the narrow boards. Is it a hairpin? Maybe a crystal from the bodice?

My heart leaps into my throat as I spot the jagged square of blood-stained glass.

This is it. The proof I've been looking for. Every website agrees, blood evidence is the best thing a case can have.

I channel years of watching crime-scene shows. Wearing a fresh pair of the disposable gloves Heather uses to do the dishes, I lift the glass with eyebrow tweezers I haven't touched in years and drop it into a sandwich baggie.

The front door opens. I bolt upright. My room looks like a goddamn crime scene. I yank off the gloves, drop the tweezers on my bed, and skitter out into the living room with the baggie still in hand, making sure to close the door behind me.

"Oh, shit!" Heather flinches. "What the hell are you doing here?"

I blink. "I live here?"

"I know that, but"—Heather presses a hand to her chest—"fuck, don't you usually have one of your doctor's appointments at five on Fridays?"

I check the clock. Five-fifteen. Which means I've already passed the late-arrival threshold, and I'll have to pay Dana's fee no matter what.

"It got canceled," I lie.

Heather frowns as she sets down her bag. "Okay. Did you reschedule it?"

"I'm working on it." I bounce on my toes, desperate to get through the small talk to the part where I can ask her to give the glass to Everett. "How was work?"

"Weird." She shakes her head. "When I walked in—fuck, Marcie, just tell me what you want to tell me."

"Sorry." I thrust the bag forward. "I got in contact with one of my friends from high school, and she offered to send me some of Ryan's stuff because I'm at that stage in the grieving process, and one of those things was my prom dress, and I found this piece of glass that definitely has his blood on it, so I was wondering if you could give it to Everett to test. I can totally get a blood sample from Ben somehow if he needs that."

Heather freezes halfway through taking one of her shoes off. "You... have a piece of bloody glass? And that's what's making you smile like that?"

I didn't even realize I was smiling. Quickly, I force my face into something more somber. "Paradoxical reaction, I guess. I've been crying for a while. But there's nothing more concrete than blood evidence, right? This is way better than the stupid pictures."

"Marce, you're scaring me." Heather finishes pulling off her shoe and takes a step closer. "Can we sit down for a second and just talk? Maybe get that therapy appointment rescheduled?"

I never told her it was therapy, but I guess once she knew how crazy I am—was?—the weekly appointments were pretty easy to put together. Still, I shake my head.

"I'm fine. I'm not crazy. I've just had a breakthrough, and I'm asking you to help me," I say. "Isn't that what friends do?"

Heather swallows hard and finally looks at the baggie I'm holding out to her. She winces and looks away just as quickly. "It is," she says slowly, "but friends also spend time together. So how about we make a deal? I'll take the glass to Everett and you come with me to his football games for the rest of the season."

I grimace. "The rest of the season?"

"For transporting blood?" There's no humor or pity in her voice. "You're lucky I only asked for the season. There's even the rivalry game coming up next month, so you might have fun."

I study Heather for a long moment. Her whole body is turned away from the glass, something the body-language experts I've been watching in between my forensic research says means someone hates something. And she's barely looked at it. But I don't have access to a lab on my own, not that I'd know what to do with it if I did.

If she doesn't hold up her end, I still have the dress. The sample should be better on the glass, but I have more.

"Okay." I hold out the baggie. "All season."

She takes it. "Starting tomorrow."

I nod. Heather tucks the baggie in her backpack then heads into the kitchen presumably to make something for dinner. I need a comparative sample, and I don't know if I can trust Heather. So I only have one option. I pull out my phone and open Ben's thread.

Okay, I say. *Just tell me when.*

2 6

IN THE LION'S DEN

MARCIE

I STAND on the front stoop of an apartment building I've seen once before trying to catch my racing breath. Ben texted me back right away and said he was free tonight. Maybe I should've expected that. Maybe I should've backed down when he asked to meet somewhere private because the explanation is kind of personal. Maybe I should've told Heather I was coming here instead of saying Dana had a late appointment open up.

But I'm so close I can taste it. A bright picture unfolds in my mind. I walk upstairs, and Ben-Ryan confesses, and he's carted off to jail where he further confesses that I never even hallucinated Ryan because he was visiting me all along. Dana apologizes and says I'm done with therapy. I change my major and get the degree in theater I wanted. Hell, I move back home, and everyone there apologizes too. I get a chance to be the person I was always meant to be, without Ben-Ryan's interference.

I buzz apartment four.

"Hi, uh, I'm downstairs," I say. "Marcie. I'm Marcie."

Thankfully, Ben only replies with thunderous footsteps pounding downstairs, and the door opens a second later.

"Hi," he says breathlessly.

Backlit like this, he barely looks like Ryan. I could be a normal girl headed in for a normal date with a normal boy. I will be, someday, when this is over. I step inside.

"Sorry about the delay." He rubs his hands on a towel over his shoulder. "I was cooking."

"I'm starving." Another lie. I'm so full of chips the warm smell of food drifting down the stairs barely tempts me. But lying to him seems safest.

"Great." He grins and gestures me up ahead of him.

I can't turn my back on him. I bow dramatically and gesture for him. "You'll find, good sir, I have no clue where we're going."

He chuckles. "Fair enough."

Up the stairs, Ben shoulders open a door, and the food smell intensifies. Rich cheese, tart tomatoes. Something Italian.

"Shoes off?" I ask. Ryan lived in an aggressively shoes-off household.

"Whatever works." Ben darts inside, headed for the small kitchen where something bubbles on the stove. He's wearing slippers.

I purse my lips and decide to leave my shoes on—in case I need to run. I shut the door behind me, and for once, check that it didn't lock. Very much still open.

"This'll be done soon," he calls over his shoulder.

"No worries." I pull off my coat and drift deeper into the apartment. "I know this was short notice."

If I had to use one word to describe the place, it would be... nondescript. The couch and kitchen table are obviously the furniture Ardent offers to lease with the apartment. There are two pieces of art on the wall. One is a black-and-white landscape I suspect might be Ansel Adams. The other is a framed, blown-up version of *Manticore Quest*'s German cover. There's a TV on a low table I swear I saw on the street at the beginning of the semester, but it's off. Only two doors dot the walls of this combined, open space, other than the one I came in through. The open one shows a sliver of a bathroom. The closed one, presumably, hides his bedroom.

He's been here for a couple of months now. Why is his home so empty?

"Ta-da!" he says.

I turn to see him ladling pasta and bright red sauce into two wide bowls.

"Pasta alla Laurel." He grins. "My mom was terrified to send me off without any cooking skills, so she taught me a few simple dishes."

Ryan's mom's name was Beverly. I sit at the kitchen table. "This doesn't look simple to me."

He laughs. "You don't cook much?"

"Some," I reply defensively. Then, I look at the dish he sets in front of me. Green herbs and pale chunks of garlic and onion poke out of the deep-red sauce, the kind of red you get when you use real tomatoes. "Okay, my specialty is grilled cheese. Fancy food hasn't been a priority."

"Try telling that to my mom." He shakes his head but doesn't sit. "I have wine. This is supposed to be better with wine."

Alcohol might loosen his tongue, but there's no way it won't affect me worse. I shake my head.

"I'll take a soda, if you have it."

He nods, grabs two cans of cola from a box inside the fridge, and finally sits. "Bon appétit."

I pick up my fork then look at him, my heart beating in my throat. "So… you offered to explain. About the scars."

His shoulders slump. "I know I freaked out, and it was unfair to you. I'm sensitive about them. And I'm really sorry. But… can we please just eat dinner first? Like normal people?"

The hair on the back of my neck prickles. Does he know about Dana, about my institutionalization? Was that a dig?

"Please?" he says.

He actually sounds fragile. Worried. Maybe that wasn't a clue.

"Okay," I say reluctantly.

"Thank you." He exhales slowly. "Now, feel free to be brutal with me about the food. Mom may have taught me, but I haven't exactly been practicing."

I take a bite, and the flavors burst over my tongue. Rich, warm, herbal and tomato-y.

"Holy shit," I say through a full mouth.

He winces. "That bad?"

"Not by a long shot." I swallow, my appetite suddenly revived. "Try it."

He twists up his own bite, then smiles in relief. "Thank God Mom's not going to disown me. Needs something though."

I shake my head. "As far as I can tell, it's perfect."

"Flattery will get you everywhere." He grins. "Except to better pasta."

"I don't give a shit," I reply. "My mom hated cooking, so I was raised on takeout and frozen dinners." Inspiration strikes. "I don't think a week went by without a trip to the Fishy."

The Fishy was the name of Etta McCreevy' restaurant, which she nearly perfectly recreated from her parents' fish and chips shop back in Ireland. Around town, we never called it anything else.

"The what?" Ben asks.

He's the picture of innocence. So perfect it must be practiced.

"Oh, a local fish and chips place." I poke at my food. "I forget that's not what they're called sometimes."

He laughs. "Fish and chips only? In Indiana? How did that end up there?"

I shouldn't have used a real story. "Oh, a local woman moved from Ireland. It was her parents' place that she recreated over here."

"Damn." Ben opens his soda and takes a sip. "The coolest restaurant we had in my hometown was a combination sushi bar-taco stand."

"What?" I ask before I can catch my curiosity.

"Oh, just you wait," he says. "Both of them were outside."

I splutter a laugh. "Maybe they should've called that the Fishy. It had to smell, right?"

"Like you wouldn't believe." He takes another bite, then smacks the table. "Lemon!"

I blink. "O…kay?"

He grabs a lemon from the wooden bowl between us and begins rolling it against the table. "Can you grab me a knife? Trust me, this'll make everything better."

I stand and head for the drawer to the left of the sink. "And why are you squishing it?"

"Releases the juice," he answers. "Sorry, I'm supposed to be cool and suave tonight. To tenderize it, baby."

I open the drawer and grab a serrated knife with a laugh. "That's your suave? I guess I don't have to worry about competition."

"I'm wounded." He accepts the knife, slices the lemon down the middle, and squeezes a little onto each of our plates. "I liked you better when you were complimenting my food."

"Let's see if there's anything to compliment." I take my seat, still the pasta, and have another bite.

Fuck me, it is better.

Ben laughs triumphantly before I say a word.

I DON'T KNOW how he does this every time, but I relax. Dinner disappears. We trade stories about our hometowns. He has a lot of them, though he's not the best with details. It takes me eight or ten stories to notice because he's an expert at covering the gaps with a dramatic reenactment or the perfect joke. When the food is gone, I don't know which of us suggests moving to the couch, but I know I don't move away when he sits right next to me.

"We could watch something," he says.

"What kind of movies do you like?" I ask.

"This and that." He yawns and stretches his arms, then drapes one of them around my shoulders.

He is warm and so close. He looks like Ryan. He might be Ryan. How do I keep letting my guard down? Am I really this stupid?

"Tell me about your scars," I blurt.

BY HEART

Ben

I FLINCH BACK from Marcie and her question. She just had to ask again, and right when I almost forgot that was why she agreed to come over. My stomach twists, and I feel like a science experiment.

But she hasn't pulled out of my hold. Her dark eyes search my face. She seems interested.

Whatever it takes to keep her. I draw in a deep breath.

"Believe it or not, I didn't spend my whole childhood inside playing weird video games," I say. "I wasn't much for team sports, but my dad got me into rock climbing. First, we did those little fake walls at gyms, back when I was nine or ten. But they got easy pretty quickly, so we moved onto real mountains." I smile grimly. "Or as close as we could come to mountains in Illinois."

Marcie furrows her brow, but she nods. I ache to smooth that little wrinkle, make her understand.

"Anyway, when I graduated from high school, my parents asked what I wanted for a present. There was this cliff just outside of town. Not a mountain, not by a long shot, but it's a YDS four." I clear my throat. "Uh, pretty tough, in climbing terms. Mostly we capped out at twos, with the rare three. Mom completely refused to let us attempt it for years. And I said that was what I wanted. To scale it just once before I moved away."

Marcie covers her mouth. "You said there was an accident—"

"Please, let me finish." I swallow against a suddenly thick throat. "We picked a day in early June. The forecast was promising, and on the day of, it was even better than we'd hoped. Cool for the season, slightly cloudy." I've looked at that forecast a thousand times because Dad printed it out on that last morning and shot it under my door as I was getting ready. Yet another piece of the past I almost brought with me but took out of my suitcase at the last second instead. "We offered for Mom to come and watch, but she said she'd be too nervous. So she stayed home, and we headed out. On the drive, Dad asked if I wanted to be the lead climber. I said yes."

"What does that mean?" Marcie asks.

Questions always make it harder. "It's not like we were climbing an unknown route—all the bolts were in place and everything—but the lead climber places any other protection and clips into those anchors." I swallow. "Basically, a good lead makes sure everyone is safe. He'd never let me do it before."

Marcie's eyes widened. I could see the pieces starting to click into place. I pulled my arm back and fiddled with the hem of my shirt.

"According to the people who found us, one of the cams—uh, this expandable thing that helps out when there are cracks in the route— just... gave. And I didn't thread his belay correctly. We both fell." I stare at my hands. "I survived–with a lot of surgery. He didn't."

Silence fills my apartment. My own pulse thrums in my ears, a constant side effect of the fall, along with serious tinnitus. And the back pain that keeps me up at night. But I said all the words correctly, I'm sure. I know the facts by heart. They were the first things I learned when I woke up in the hospital, nearly three days after the accident. Finally, I can't take it anymore. I look up at Marcie.

I don't see pity on her face. Or shock. Most of the people I told, back in the first couple years of college, switched between those two.

No, she looks almost… calculating? Like she's trying to do a complicated math problem in her head.

"You said this was your graduation present," she says. "So you were eighteen?"

"Uh, yeah." I frown. "Just, actually. My birthday's in May."

"And this was in Illinois." She almost sounds like she's talking to herself. "What was the name of the cliff? They have names, right?"

"Kramer's Spit," I reply. "Why?"

"Just curious." She shakes her head. "I'm sorry. I forgot to say I was sorry, and that's awful."

That's more normal. "Thanks."

"Can I ask"—she glances at me—"was it just your head that got injured?"

I pick at the hem of my shirt more aggressively. "No. Are these details important? I don't love talking about this."

"Of course not. I'm sorry." She grimaces. "Just one last thing?"

Whatever it takes. I nod.

"The last time we talked about this, you seemed really casual. But… I mean, your dad was right next to you, right? Did you, like, lose consciousness or something right away?" She peers at me. "Because otherwise, I can't imagine how you laughed about it."

Moment of truth. I take one of her hands—she lets me, but she doesn't hold on tight—and stare into her eyes.

"Do you like me?" I ask. "Like, do you want to keep seeing each other? Stay in my life?"

The question seems to startle her. Her eyebrows fly up, and her mouth opens slightly. Great. Scott was right, and I am coming on too strong, and I've officially blown this.

I start to release her hand. "Sorry—"

"No!" She holds me in place, then clears her throat. "I mean, no, don't pull back. I… I think I do. Like you."

I study her face. She gnaws on her lip, but she meets my gaze when I seek out her eyes. Conflicted, but not conflicted enough to run away. Maybe she's alarmed by my story. Maybe she's just not very emotionally available. I haven't found anyone other than Heather that she's close with. So it would make sense that her fumbling confession means more from her than it would from someone else.

Or maybe I want it to. Maybe I'm a sucker who's already in too deep. But fuck it, I want this to mean something. So I open my mouth and tell her the thing I haven't admitted to a stranger in nearly four years now.

"I don't know. I don't remember the accident." I suck in a breath. "Or a second of the eighteen years before it."

28

UNMOORED

Marcie

My mouth drops open. He doesn't remember anything? A whole childhood, just missing?

"But you told so many stories," I say.

"Secondhand." He shrugs. "Familiar things were supposed to help me regain my memories, so most of those first few weeks were just Mom pumping me full of stories about myself between sobbing fits."

"Fuck." I sink back against the couch. I lost eighteen years, too, but more like if I'd lost the sweater Grandma bought me one Christmas that I absolutely hated by "accidentally" leaving it on the bus. He really lost it. I can't imagine having so much *nothing* to look back on. Even just hearing about it, I feel like a boat set out to sea, lost and drifting.

"The people who found you… they're all you know about the accident?"

He nods. What a stupid question. I don't even know what I'm asking anymore.

"Your life starts in the hospital," I murmur.

"Hey, don't worry." He smiles. "The life I don't remember started in St. Mary Medical too. I was born there, or so I've been told."

"I don't remember where I was born either," I say, half-hysterical.

He laughs. Just like he did last time I asked him about this. Maybe a little more earnestly, where the last time was almost defensive. Deflective. Is this why so many of his stories have holes in them? Why he's so good at patching them over with a smile and a joke? Why he seems to swing wildly between confident and awkward? He's had to relearn himself in pieces, and clearly, he's still learning.

This means Ryan could've survived, part of me argues. *Falling off a mountain has to be worse than getting hit by an SUV.*

I don't know that. I can't know that. And, fuck, neither can he.

I've been quiet for way too long.

"Does it hurt?" I blurt. "Still?"

Ben sighs. "Are you asking about the injuries or my dad?"

Maybe the worst possible question. He lost a parent he literally can't remember. How do you grieve that? My ribs start to crush into my lungs, and I shrug, my tongue no longer online.

"Yeah to both, I guess." He looks away, over the back of the couch. "I'm told I used to sleep a lot better."

Suddenly, everything I've been doing this past week feels monstrous. On the off chance this random man is my dead best friend, he wouldn't even know. There are no clues to find, no secrets to uncover. Just a guy who lost everything.

And the crazy girl who latched onto him.

All my evidence turns to sand in my fingers. He takes a lot of pictures of women with dark hair, the absolute most common hair color. He has a protective mom, like a probably shocking amount of people. He bashed his head in and survived, which might be rare but is nothing more than a freak coincidence. My mind replays the moment I burst in on Heather and Everett, the look they exchanged. Do the pictures even look similar? I've certainly been known to see things no one else can.

My ribs collapse into my lungs. My heart hammers. Holy shit. I walked in here thinking I was about to prove I'd been sane all along, and instead, I find out that I'm so much crazier than I feared.

"Hey." Ben squeezes my hand. I forgot he had that. "Look at me."

I drag my gaze up to his face. It looks so much like Ryan's. But maybe I just pushed myself too hard with a full slate of classes, and I saw what I wanted to see.

"I get that this can be intense." He rubs his thumb in small circles on my skin. "Trust me, being 'born' at eighteen doesn't exactly make for a normal college experience. But... I don't know the guy who fell off that cliff."

"What?" I blink back sudden tears.

"It's hard to explain." He smiles ruefully. "It's like... okay, you said you have someone you don't like to remember, right?"

It takes me a second, but finally, I remember that's how I described Ryan to him. I nod.

"So, there's the version of you who knew them, or was close to them, or whatever you were, and then there's the version after; you don't want to remember them anymore. Two versions of you separated by one incident."

He's far more correct than he could even imagine. Tears press against the backs of my eyes, begging for release.

"I like to think of him like that. He's the Ben who went up. I'm the Ben who came down." That rueful smile returns. "I don't want an old me, one I don't even remember, to consume my whole life. Like you don't want to keep being defined by memories of that person. The Ben who came down is the one who's here." He shrugs. "The one who's real, if you want to get into meta crap."

I take a long breath as his words strike a chord in my chest. My pretty visions of becoming un-crazy, of rewriting time to become the person I was going to be before Ryan's death, fall to pieces. And somehow, I don't mind. In pieces, I can see the vision for the useless pipe dream it was. Lily Nelson walked into prom. Or maybe into the institution. Maybe both. But regardless, Marcie Holt walked out, and I can't ever get Lily back. I shouldn't want to.

I've had so many new experiences, learned so much, changed and grown. Lily wouldn't have had the balls to march in here thinking she might be attacked by a homicidal undead Ryan. Hell, Lily wouldn't have had the balls to stay in Ben's lap that first night and flirt, alcohol or no alcohol. She was in love with Ryan for years, and she never said a word. Lily walked out on her living best friend and never looked back. And I spent the first five years of being Marcie trying to figure out how to be Lily again. What a waste.

"Does that make sense?" Ben asks quietly.

"Yes," I breathe. "Thank you."

When his mouth opens in surprise, I don't think twice before leaning in.

I don't have a plan. But he makes a low noise in the back of his throat, and suddenly, I know exactly where this night is going. My body lights like a power grid that hasn't been turned on in a long time, flickering in places but coursing with energy. I kiss him hungrily.

He rises to the occasion. Like he's gotten more comfortable since we made out just a week ago, his movements are a little surer. He pushes his tongue against my lips this time, and I part for him easily. When he doesn't seem to quite know what to do from there, I paint suggestions with my own tongue. He tastes like the cola we both drank, intoxicatingly sticky-sweet. And I need more. I take the hand I'm holding and put it on my waist, under my shirt.

Ben pulls back. "I don't want to go too fast."

I flush. "Yeah, of course. You're probably tired."

"No, you're—" He shakes his head. "Last time we jumped in like this, it ended badly. And I really don't want this to end badly."

My chest warms. "Me neither. So, what, want to stick to second base?"

His blue eyes go nearly black as his pupils dilate. "How far were you thinking?"

"Home run?" My face is on fire. Usually, I throw myself at someone, and we fall into bed. I don't know what to do with all this talking.

"I like you." He swallows visibly. "And I want the… home run to be special. If that's not too cheesy."

Fuck. I've never hooked up with anyone like this. "Um, okay."

Ben drags his gaze up and down my body. "How about we go to the bedroom, get comfortable, take it slow, and see where the night leads us?"

I stand silently with his hand still in mine. My words seem to be failing me a lot tonight.

2 9

LEAP OF FAITH

MARCIE

BEN LEADS me to the final door, the one I guessed hid his bedroom.

"Shoes off." He smiles sheepishly and kicks off his slippers.

I untie my sneakers. He opens the door. Inside, the walls are also soft beige, and the furniture looks like rental stuff, but I barely notice anything other than his patient gaze on me. I'm not a power grid anymore. I'm something warmer, softer. I remove my shoes, and he pulls me inside the room.

Then, because it's him, he fumbles for a few minutes. The light level isn't right, so he puts on a lamp instead. It's too quiet, so he plays some music then changes the playlist three times. I lie on the bed, watching him, that warm feeling growing all the while.

Quickly, before I forget, I text Heather that I headed to the library after my session and not to expect me home soon.

Finally, Ben turns to me, his eyes dark. I pat the mattress. He ignores the instruction and climbs on top of me instead, coaxing a surprised gasp from my lips. With a smile, he kisses me.

Without the pressure of a destination, our kisses stretch out, slow and languorous. I've never made out with anyone like this before, like we're trying to learn every inch of each other before going further. It's strangely vulnerable, even as his stiffening cock between us promises he wants me as much as I want him. I do slip my hands up under his shirt to find surprising muscle under there. Climber's muscle, maybe. He moves in a way I'm not expecting, and my short nails scrape across his skin.

He groans, and a few lights in that power grid flicker to life.

"Touch me," I find myself saying. "Please."

"Put your hands in my hair," he replies.

I didn't even realize I was avoiding that, but it becomes obvious as soon as he says the words. Despite everything, the latticework of scars scares me a little. My heart thuds as I slide one hand out of his shirt, up his chest, and into his mop of blond hair.

There are so many more scars than I thought. Long and short, fat and thin, straight and jagged. They paint a gruesome picture of a day the man who owns them can't remember. The room starts to go wavy as I struggle to breathe.

Ben kisses me. No one in my mind kisses like this, so it must be real. I hold onto his hair and lose myself in the pressure of his mouth.

Long moments later, he tugs on the bottom of my shirt. I sit up obligingly, and he pulls the fabric slowly out of the way, leaving our chests pressed together. Despite my bra, I need to feel him. I yank his shirt up too, and he chuckles as it goes. His fine, golden chest hair brushes the tops of my breasts. I sigh shakily.

Ben presses me back down into the bed and palms my breasts through my bra. I arch up into him, panting. Already, I want to ask for more. But he wants to take this slow. He wants to know me. So I endure this touch so close to where I want it for thirty breaths, what I would call an admirable effort, before reaching behind myself to unclasp the underwear keeping me from what I really want.

When I pull it away, Ben sits up. I think I'm about to get another speech about moving slow, but he just… looks. He traces a delicate finger along the outside curve of one breast. His mouth is almost thoughtful.

"Beautiful," he murmurs.

Before I have time to blush, he crushes himself onto me again and begins using his mouth. Clearly, he's not as experienced in this. He bites down too hard on a nipple, and I wince.

"Sorry." He looks up at me. "Can you tell me what you want?"

I don't know what I want. My drunken party days didn't yield memorable sex, even if it was good at the time, and he just shoved in my face how long I've spent running away.

"Or what feels good," he adds.

That, I can maybe do. I am fully in my body for the first time in I don't even know how long. I nod and anchor my hand in his hair, growing used to the texture of the scars. Ben leans back in.

"Too sharp."

"Left, I think."

"Circles."

"Oh, fuck, like that."

He takes direction well, even my shitty direction, and before long, I'm writhing. I couldn't tell him what to do if I wanted to, but he seems to have picked up the gist. Even through my jeans, I can tell I'm soaked. If he backs off here, I'll be getting myself off alone tonight. I clutch his hair, my only anchor in this storm of sensation.

Ben looks up at me with heavy-lidded eyes. "I'd really like to fuck you."

"Yes," I gasp. "Please."

He opens his nightstand and shuffles around until he finds a condom while I shimmy off my sticky pants and underwear. He does stop dead for a second when he turns back, staring again, and I do my best to let him. I'm not really beautiful, but it's hard not to believe he's attracted to me when he looks like that. Then, he clears his throat and begins to take off his pants.

I pluck the condom out of his fingers and open it. His pants and boxers fall, and his cock springs out proudly. Long, but not too thick. My mouth waters. I have to focus. Before he can stop me, I position the condom, pinch the tip, and slide it on torturously slowly. He groans, and I smile.

"Need any more help?" I ask.

He blinks desire-hazed eyes into a little more clarity. "I mean, if there's anything specific you want—"

He's so sweet, so earnest, that I have to pull him in for another kiss before the warmth in my chest overwhelms me completely. Luring him back onto the bed, back on top of me, is easy. I don't know what I want other than him, but I get the sense he'll let me experiment. When we're lying back, I line him up with my entrance and hook a leg around his hips.

"Are you sure you're ready?" he asks.

I pull him forward. The familiar burn of the stretch welcomes me, coaxes a moan from my lips. Ben moans in harmony. He's not fully hilted yet, but he lingers for a moment, like he's just enjoying the sensation. Like I'm a good meal he intends to savor. I pull with my leg, but he resists with a strength I don't expect. The pace is his now.

A split second of panic flashes through me as I lose control of the situation. Then, he looks at me with an aching softness. There's not a hint of malevolence in those eyes.

Even if he was Ryan, he wouldn't know. There's no scheme, no mystery. Just a normal-ish girl and a normal-ish guy having sex. I exhale, and he sinks deeper like he was waiting for me to relax.

Ben fucks me just as slowly and thoughtfully as he kissed me. My orgasm threatens as he speeds up, fades as he slows back down again. It should be agonizing. I let myself float away in it. My body is nothing but pleasure, and I'll take that after the last six years.

"Come for me," he says suddenly.

I can't help it. I laugh. "Yeah, it doesn't work like that in real life."

"I had a girlfriend—" He purses his lips. "Okay. Tell me what you need."

I guide his hand in between my legs to my clit. "Circles. Not directly on it. In rhythm, if you can manage it."

Ben kisses me, slow and sweet, and circles his thumb around my clit. Every circuit in the power grid lights immediately, like a flash of lightning.

"Fuck," he groans. "You're incredible."

He begins moving again, and I can do nothing but cling to him as senseless noises pour from my lips. My orgasm races forward with all the threatening force of a bullet train.

"Now," I gasp.

Ben crushes himself closer to me as I spasm, hilted finally, every inch of my skin touching his. My vision goes white. His name is on my lips. Only when I start to come back down do I realize he followed me over the edge. Like he was waiting.

When the aftershocks run out, I look up at him. I know what happens now. He runs off to dump the condom, then says something about an early class or roommates or whatever excuse he needs to get me out of here.

Instead, he smiles. "I don't suppose you want to find out how good I am at breakfast?"

30

SMOOTH SAILING

I DRUM on the corner table at Fitzgerald's, a little restaurant off campus Marcie and I have been going to a lot over the past three weeks of dating.

Three weeks. That still feels crazy to say. Three amazing weeks of dinners out, evenings in my apartment, stolen moments after class. Well, fewer of those. She pretty much insists that we spend time in my apartment or off campus. But she has a roommate, and I don't, so I'm fairly sure that's normal. And things are so easy with her, even after my confession. She looks at me like I've grown a second head every now and again, but those moments are getting fewer and farther between. I'm hopeful they'll disappear entirely before too long. We're just getting used to each other, a little more every time we hang out.

And she'll be here soon. I run my hands through my hair. The wind kind of wrecked it. I really should wear a hat as the temperature drops, but somehow I only brought one from home, and I haven't been able to find it in like a week.

The door opens, and Marcie walks in looking equally wind ruffled. Her dark hair, loose from its braid like she seems to prefer for dates, splays in every direction like a halo. The high pink spots on her cheeks and brightness in her eyes are so stunningly alive my hand itches for a camera. Someday, I'll get her to model for me again. But I want to make sure she knows I like her for more than her beauty.

She catches my eye and hurries over to the table, shucking off her coat. Underneath, she wears a long-sleeved sweater dress I haven't seen before that hugs her every curve. My mouth goes dry. A second ago, I was starving, but maybe dinner is optional.

"Sorry I'm late." She drops onto the bench across from me. "Got caught up in homework. I know I should've texted."

"And what if Sir Lancival had shown up late with some weak excuse about texting?" I smile teasingly so she knows I'm not hurt.

"Then he would've married Morgengraun in disguise, and the kingdom would've fallen." She sighs heavily, then takes my hand and winks. "Thank God you only have to worry about not having gotten your breadsticks yet."

I laugh, and the waiter comes over to take our orders.

"So then Theresa swings the pool noodle down like it's a sword of death and—" Marcie stops abruptly. "Someone charged in, and we started playing chicken. Sorry, I thought that story was more interesting."

I look up from my nearly empty plate and study her suddenly pale face. After three weeks, I've figured out all these dead stops in her stories are places where the person she doesn't want to remember go. The first time I asked, she clammed up and left the date early, so I've just been leaving them alone. But things have been going great. Better than any of my other relationships. We've hung out like three times a week since that first night, and tonight, we've nearly finished our meal without her releasing my hand. And anyway, we started this relationship with my biggest secret. I think it's time.

"That someone is the person you don't want to think about, right?" I say gently.

Marcie clenches her jaw. "Yeah. Maybe. Uh—"

I squeeze her hand. "Can you tell me about them? At least whether I'm supposed to hate them or feel sad or something else?"

She pushes the remains of her meatloaf around her plate for a long moment. My pulse throbs in my ears. I might've blown tonight. She's so hard to read, no matter how much attention I pay. It's infuriating and intriguing.

She glances up at me with a soft, shy smile. "He was my best friend."

My stomach swoops. "Was?"

She nods. "I would say he falls firmly in the 'sad' category over 'hate.' He, uh, died during prom. They cremated him before I even graduated."

I blow out a breath. "Shit. I'm sorry."

"Me too." She squeezes my hand. "You would've liked him. We were obsessed with *Manticore Quest* together."

"Sounds like my kind of guy." I laugh, half to lighten the mood and half in relief. Maybe it's selfish, but I'm a little glad a guy who makes her smile like that isn't walking around, waiting for his moment. I wouldn't stand a chance.

"Remembering him is tough." She shrugs.

I kiss her cheek, and she turns her head so I can capture her mouth. Just for a moment—we really don't want to get kicked out of this restaurant—but she needs to know how much I care about her. That I understand even these few details were tough for her.

"Thank you," I say.

"He rode his own pool noodle in like it was a horse," she replies. "With another for a lance."

"Now you have to keep telling me stories about him." I grin.

I RUB Marcie's shoulder on the couch in my living room, some old movie she likes blaring on my TV. When I asked her to come back to my place after dinner, I expected her to say no because of the best friend talk. My dick has some very specific thoughts about what her "yes" might mean, but I'm just happy to have her next to me where I can inhale her flowery shampoo and feel her warmth.

She makes a soft noise in her throat and snuggles in. I know, if I tip her face up to mine, we'll be having sex on the couch a few minutes later. With Marcie, the first kiss is like lighting a match. And I can't deny, I like knowing how much she wants me. But her slow relaxation is so much more interesting to me. I feel like every time we hang out, she reveals a new piece of herself to me. I want to know her even more than I want her body.

Even in that dress.

The movie drones on, and my eyelids start to droop. Not exactly cool-guy behavior to fall asleep in the middle of the date, so I force my eyes open. Then, Marcie makes another small sound. A different one. I jerk up to look at her.

Her mouth is slack, her eyes shut. She makes the noise again. A snore. She's dead asleep, her head pillowed on my shoulder. My heart hums.

The next time my eyelids fall, I don't fight them.

I STARE UP INTO BLACKNESS. There's something there, I know. A monster in the night.

"Please." I know I'm speaking, but my voice is higher than I've ever heard it. "Please, don't."

My heart hammers in my throat. I want to fight, but I can't see the monster, and it's so much bigger than me. I'm so small. It laughs, low and rumbling.

There! A shape in all black against the darkness. The monster moves, and its claws glint in light I can't see.

"Don't shoot my dad," I sob.

~

SOMEONE SHAKES MY SHOULDER. I blink awake with a bright burst of panic.

"Whoa!" Marcie leans back. "Sorry, didn't mean to startle you."

As quickly as it came, the panic is gone again. Weird. I rub my eyes.

"No, I'm sorry. What's up?"

Marcie holds up her phone to show the time. Twelve-forty-five. "I have to get home before Heather freaks."

We haven't been able to organize a sleepover since that first night. And I have to call Mom anyway. I kiss the side of Marcie's head.

"Get home safe. Text me when you're there."

She nods and begins packing up. I rub my chest, chasing the ghost of a feeling I already can't remember.

31

CRAZY IN... LIKE?

"You seem to be in a good mood lately," Dana says. "Anything in particular inspiring that?"

I blink. "Am I? I hadn't noticed."

A lie, and a stupid one. I've kind of been walking on air since getting together with Ben, though I don't know whether that's about Ben himself or what he said. I've just been focusing on being Marcie—without the pressure of having been Lily–and it's seriously freeing. I don't spend all my time worrying about what people think about me. I wear what I want because I want to. I even told Heather to forget about the blood—because I claimed Dana said forensic testing wasn't acceptance—but promised to go to the games with her anyway. Being surrounded by people is a lot more fun when I don't spend the whole time wondering if they can tell I'm crazy.

Dana flips back a few pages in her notebook. "I would say so. I keep loose track of my patients' moods, as well as the number of positive versus negative things they say in a session, and both of yours took a strong upswing about three weeks ago."

My heart leaps into my throat. Before my second date with Ben, I told Dana I was seeing someone, just not who. If she looks far enough back in her notes to find that, I'm in trouble.

"I mean, fall is my favorite season." I cuddle into my favorite light-weight sweater, perfect for transitioning into the pseudo-chill of Virginia winters. "It's much easier to be positive when walking outside every morning doesn't feel like getting slapped in the face with a warm, wet towel."

"I can't disagree, but you don't usually show such a pronounced mood shift at this time of year. If we go back—" She starts to turn more pages.

"Maybe it's my classes," I blurt.

Dana looks up at me. "You haven't spoken about those much. I was wondering about them."

"They're actually going great." Thankfully, true, now that I've gotten my head out of my ass about the whole stupid Ben-Ryan thing. "I'm on track to get A's in everything."

"That's amazing." Dana smiles. "What do you think made the difference this semester?"

Fuck, she's still circling. I fidget with one of the pillows next to me.

"Time." I nod seriously. "I think you were right, and I just needed time to distance myself from the, uh, grief."

She peers at me, her green eyes sharp. "Have you been sleeping well? You usually only use filler words like that when you're particularly tired or...."

The end of her sentence looms between us. Or I'm caught off guard, hiding something.

"I guess my sleep schedule hasn't been the best." I toss in a yawn. "Four classes of homework is more than I'm used to, and I've been staying up later than usual to keep on top of it."

She makes a few notes. "Maybe I reach out to your psychiatrist, see if we can't get sleeping pills added to your regimen."

"No," I say quickly. "I'll just try to manage my workload better. It's not an issue that medication would help with."

Dana hums. "Marcie, you know this only works if you're honest with me."

"I know." And I do. I feel so stupid lying to her like this. I just know how it looks. She'd think I'm indulging, no matter how many times I explain I'm doing the exact opposite.

"So, do you have anything else you want to talk to me about?" she asks.

"Uh...." I do. Of course I do. I want to brag about my new boyfriend and how happy he makes me. I want to talk about my roommate and how sick to my stomach lying to her makes me. Heather thinks I'm going out on a string of app dates, trying to put myself back out there after the mess with Ben. Or that I'm really studying hard, depending on whether I think I've "gone out" too much that week or not. Every time I come home, she asks me excitedly about my latest man, and I make up a new story. I've started trolling lists of romance novels and just stealing the descriptions of the heroes. It's exhausting, and I feel like a monster. But just like Dana, she won't understand. If I was on the outside, I wouldn't! And I don't want to lose the friendship we're building. So I'll just wait until some time has passed, maybe a semester, in which I'm as stable as Ben makes me, then tell her. She'll see the difference then. Maybe I'll do the same with Dana.

Her phone pings, the usual reminder for the end of our session.

"Nope!" I say. "Or at least, nothing that can't wait until next time."

She purses her lips. "Please feel free to contact me between sessions if you need to. I can always move things around in my schedule."

"I absolutely will." I shoulder my backpack and stride out the door. After a short elevator ride, I emerge into the bright fall sunlight. I really do love this season.

With a bounce in my step, I type a quick text to Theresa, asking if she's available for another call soon. We've been talking once a week since she sent the box, and I've really missed her.

She's also the only one who knows about Ben. She's not happy about it, but she can't stop me from all the way over in Indiana. And I think I'm getting through to her about why this is good for me. Maybe.

I tuck my phone away and focus on enjoying the day around me. The first few leaves crunch underfoot, and there's a nip in the air that promises falling temperatures soon. And, of course, plastered on every bulletin board and telephone pole are flyers for the upcoming rivalry game. There's nowhere I can turn without seeing Ardent blue against Bennett purple or an Ardent alligator snarling at a cowering Bennett bear. Every other year, I've rolled my eyes at the posters and written down which day I have to make sure to stay inside. This year, I'm actually kind of excited to be going. I just wish I could invite Ben. I can picture him either being the slouchy, anti-spirit guy or the one who shows up with his whole body painted blue and screams the whole time.

In the end, I think the worst part of hiding him from everyone might be how much time we have to spend apart. Everett is over at the apartment all the time, but I won't even let Ben step inside the complex. One time, he cornered me after class, and it took all the willpower I had to only kiss him once and send him away. My heart thuds unevenly whenever I think about him. At night, I go to sleep missing him.

I might be crazy—ha!—but I also might really be falling for him.

3 2

THAT'S NOT TRUE

Marcie

"Oh my God, I told you not to get in a fight on the forum." I laugh as I trudge up the stairs after another long day of classes, looking forward to having the apartment to myself.

"Tell the forum not to be wrong!" Ben replies. "I replayed my game last night just to make sure. Morgengraun never *says* they're in Camelot. It's a Mandala effect!"

"*Mandela* effect." I correct him, grinning. "Maybe it's good they keep you behind the camera instead of typing."

"Ooh, big talk from the nurse. Aren't you just doctors who couldn't hack it?"

I shove my key into the door. Despite how harsh Ben's words sound, I can still hear him laughing as quickly as he can, trying to hide his distraction in the middle of the *Arkly* offices. It's crazy to me how quickly we understand each other. How easy it is to rib each other and know no harm is intended.

"Ah, close," I say. "Doctors are actually people who wanted to be nurses but needed like a thousand more tests to be allowed in the

163

same buildings as me." I shoulder open the door. "Ah, fuck, I left the lights on this morning."

"Not exactly giving nurses a great name," he says.

"Fuck off." I drop my bag by the door. "So, for Thursday—"

"Marcie?" Heather says.

I shoot up. Yup, there's Heather, leaning over the back of the bright orange couch like I don't know she should be at work right now. Work with Ben, actually.

I hold up a finger to indicate I'm on the phone, and she nods.

"For Thursday, I was thinking I'd call after class." I untie my shoes like everything is normal.

"What?" Ben asks. "We're meeting at the restaurant, aren't we?"

"Yeah, *Theresa*, I can wait until after Teddy goes down for his nap," I reply sharply.

"Gotcha." Ben sighs. "Talk soon, okay?"

"Talk soon." I hang up and turn to Heather, my stomach churning. I hate lying to her. I hate that I can't spend the next hour on the phone with my boyfriend. "What are you doing home?"

She sighs. "Fucking *Scott* sent all the reporters home early today. Just for no reason."

I stuff my head in my bag to hide my frown. Ben was interrupted twice while we were talking, both times by people I know from Heather are reporters. Is she lying to me?

"Cool." I grab my laptop out of my backpack and head for the couch. "I was just gonna hang out until you got home anyway, so I guess we can just hang out together now. How was your day?"

"Eh, fine." She shakes her head, setting her blonde ponytail bouncing. "I didn't exactly crush my last assignment for Wittengard—uh, one of my journalism professors—so I'm trying to blow him out of the water with this next one, but I'm hitting a wall."

I click my tongue sympathetically. "That always sucks. What's the assignment?"

"Find an old news story from your hometown and rewrite it according to modern journalistic standards." She rolls her eyes. "Extra points depending upon how far back you go."

"Damn." I join her on the couch and open my laptop. The first website that pops up is one for a festival I was thinking about inviting Ben to, and I close out of it with my heart hammering. "Well, let me know if there's anyth—"

"Actually." She turns to me with her eyes glowing. "There totally is!"

"Okay?" She seems really excited for homework help, but I'm probably just keyed up from her surprising me. Probably. "What is it?"

"So, I come from bumfuck nowhere Oklahoma," she says.

"I think I drove through there once." I smile, trying to lighten the mood.

She obliges me with a snort. "And we literally got a newspaper like, ten years ago for the town. So… could I pretend I'm from your hometown and take a look at the stuff that happened there?"

My heart skips a beat. She's home at a weird time, and now she's asking specific questions about my personal life? We definitely talk more than we used to, but I didn't even realize she was from Oklahoma. This is weird.

No. That's paranoia, and Lily was the paranoid one. Or early Marcie. Either way, I don't have to be cr—*paranoid* anymore. I trust Heather. Enough to give her my real hometown, not my fake one.

"Uh, yeah." I bite my nail. "I'm from Dillsboro, Indiana."

"Cute!" She types it in. "You're a lifesaver, Marce."

See, there's proof I'm reading into things. Because if something was really happening, Heather wouldn't use the word "lifesaver" so casually. She would've noticed me being on the phone with Ben and my freakout. So I'm just reading into things.

Which means it would be totally normal to go do homework in my room instead of watching Heather twirl the end of her ponytail around one finger. She's not going to do anything. What could she even do with just my hometown? I put my hand on my laptop and will myself to close it. Nothing to see, Marcie. Sticking around would just be indulging, and while my relationship with Dana is far from the best right now, I'm starting to think she might've been right about the whole indulging thing. In some ways.

"Holy shit," Heather says. "That's your Ryan."

My heart slams into my mouth. I'm off the couch in a second, crouched on the floor next to her. The headline is bold and jarring.

Freak Car Accident Kills Local Teen, Police Slam Lax Prom Security.

I didn't even know they printed something about Ryan. Something other than his obituary, at least.

"That's him, right?" Heather points to a grainy, black-and-white copy of Ryan's senior picture.

"Yeah," I say. The room starts to go wavy around me.

"Catch up, Lil!" Ryan jogs backward down the tile hall.

"What, are they going to use up all the good backdrops?" My new heels clack on the floor as I try to reach him.

Deep breath. I'm Marcie. I don't need to be Lily anymore. I just need to know absolutely everything ever printed about this.

I skim the article. The details are stark, nothing like the flashes of oversaturated color I remember. My stomach churns as the details float past.

South Dearborn High senior... survived by his mother Beverly... outside of the Morrow Hotel... The couple involved—

"Hey, wait a minute." My tongue is thick, and my words sound slow. "They got that wrong?"

Heather peers at me then at the screen. "What?"

"There, the last line." I point with a shaking finger, then read. "The husband and wife involved in the accident are at this time not being prosecuted for a"—the words catch, but I'm not crazy, so I force them out—"a hit-and-run because, while they left the scene of the accident, they called nine-one-one before their departure."

I look at Heather. Her face shimmers, ripples, does the worm.

"That's not true."

33

A NIGHT TO REMEMBER

Lily

I grab another rock from the pile next to me and try to skip it over the drainage "river" below the bridge. Skip, skip, *splash*. As always. No matter what I do, I can't get the fucking wrist movement right. In a fit of frustration, I shove the rest of the rocks into the water at once. The water splashes up, dampening the soft pink hem of the dress I thought was so stupidly beautiful when I put it on this afternoon, and I don't even care. I stand up, wobbling in my heels, and turn to face the Morrow Hotel.

God, I didn't even walk far enough away that I can't see the lights through the, like, six trees that separates me from my prom. *My* prom! What the hell am I even doing out here? I should go back.

The thought makes me nauseous enough that I grab the banister of the teeny-tiny bridge to stay upright. Honestly, I don't know what's making me sicker, the veritable mountain of fried shrimp Theresa and I collectively housed, or the way Michaela Tucker has been throwing herself at Ryan all night. Everybody from here to Cincinnati can tell that she thinks she's getting lucky on prom night.

I snort. What a fucking stereotype. Thank God Theresa was there to spin some bullshit about *needing* to see the quarterback for the last time when Michaela pet his fucking hair, and I nearly blew chunks on her shoes.

Whatever. I'll just spend prom with my other best friend and let Ryan regret that he wasted his last chance to dance with me in high school when he's old and fat. Maybe I'll even keep all the DVDs he left at my house this year instead of turning them over on his birthday like usual.

I turn back to the Morrow Hotel, petty and pleased, just in time to see Ryan walking up the path toward me. This time, when I grab the banister, it's not nausea making my knees weak. The soft moonlight snarls in his warm, blond hair. His blue eyes shine like I imagine the ocean is going to when we finally make it to LA .Or maybe it'll be New York City. Wherever we're going. Because as pissed as I am at him right now, there's no question of a "we." Not when he wears one of the first suits I've ever seen him in, a rich navy blue that brings out his eyes and makes him look like a cross between a super-spy and a director already on his first red carpet.

Not for the first time, I thank my lucky stars Michaela Tucker is going to a school in Texas.

"Hey." Ryan jogs up to me. "I just found Theresa attempting to convince Leon Clayton to wear her like a scarf, and she said you were sick. All good?"

I offer him a shy smile and nod. "Just needed a little air."

"Great." His relief is palpable. Seems palpable. Like his prom actually does depend on me. Then, he looks back over his shoulder at the hotel. "We should get back. Michaela's really dedicated to the photo booth, so she's expecting me back for a cowboy-themed spread after this 'bathroom break.'" He smiles like that's not the worst thing I've ever heard.

I shouldn't have thrown all the rocks in the river. I should've thrown some at him. My smile sours.

"Don't let me hold you up then," I say tightly. "I can't imagine surviving prom without putting a fifteenth jackass hat on my head."

"What the fuck are you talking about?" he demands.

I flip my thin shawl over my shoulder. "I just need a little more air. Wouldn't want to keep your *girlfriend* waiting."

"Okay, you've been a dick all night." He steps onto the bridge with me. "And you know I'm only here with Michaela because you and Theresa said you were each other's dates. I couldn't be the only loser sitting alone."

"That was a joke, and you know it, Ryan Evers." I don't look at him.

"I asked if you liked Michaela." He takes another step closer. "She was my mom's fucking idea, Lil, and I asked if you thought I should take her, and you said sure. So what the hell is your problem now? Because you're really starting to ruin prom."

Something inside me snaps. I whirl on him.

"I'm ruining prom?" I laugh derisively. "*I'm* ruining prom? You don't have a goddamn leg to stand on, talking about T and the fucking quarterback when Michaela's been trying to climb inside your suit all night." I meet his gaze—stupid mistake, Ryan's eyes have always been the prettiest in the moonlight—and my mouth runs away with me. "Of course I lied about liking her. That's what you do when your *best friend* wants to take some random chick to prom who could never deserve him if she wanted to!"

Silence fills the tiny park. Tinny music just barely reaches across the street, hollow club beats filling the air between us. Ryan looks at me–and looks, and looks.

"You've got crap timing." He turns on his heel and storms away.

I've completely lost the plot. Shit, if I thought I was sick before, my stomach is trying to climb out through my mouth now. Hot tears gather in my eyes, and my face burns. Years pretending I didn't like Ryan like that, all flushed down the drain because I ate some weird shrimp and went to prom with someone else. Stupid.

But not stupid enough yet. I kick off my heels and stumble after him.

"I didn't mean it like that!" I yell.

"The hell you did," he snaps. "We've been friends for twelve years, Lil, you can't lie to me now."

"You are such a dickhead!" I screech, holding my skirt in both hands so I can run through the thin tree cover to keep up. "You know Michaela's a mistake. Stop running away and face me like a fucking man!"

"Fine!" Ryan turns back to me. Nothing exists except his face, half in shadow and half in the yellow lights of the hotel. I've never seen him look so hurt. "Think I'm making a mistake all you want. But I'm not going to miss my goddamn—"

The bright, white light looms around the turn. He's in the middle of the fucking road. Something screeches. Brakes? I open my mouth, try to scream.

But I've always had shitty timing. My vocal cords freeze into a single chunk of ice.

The front of the black SUV hits Ryan like a battering ram. He goes up so high into the air. A distant, wild part of me remembers those old cartoons, hopes he won't fall if he just doesn't look down.

I will never forget the sound of Ryan hitting the pavement as long as I live.

Time resumes its normal pace. Blood spatters like it never does in movies, in every direction, hot and red and tasting like iron. My hands shake around my skirt. He didn't even have time to scream. He's just lying there. I can barely see him through the trees, his suit stained red like everything else in the night.

His chest rises and falls once, unevenly, and I think the world might keep spinning. I just barely claw back enough control over my body to shut my eyes. The sound of the fucking engine, the engine that hit him, fills the night. I can't leave him alone with that engine and the monster behind it.

I wrench my eyes open again.

Someone has their arm under Ryan's shoulder, heaving him off the ground. The monster is helping. No, monsters. A second shape moves in the darker, slower, but they do catch Ryan when the first monster stumbles. I have to scream, to tell them I'm here, that I know his blood type and his medical history and everything else the hospital will need to help him.

I don't move. I don't know if I have a body anymore.

The two monsters cross in front of the one working headlight. Both of them have dark ponytails. Women.

Now, Lily, I coax. *Now! Before he leaves without you!*

The two women put him in the vehicle and drive away. I'm still standing, frozen, in the thin, fake woods when Mrs. Lambert races out to check on the noise someone heard and starts screaming.

3 4

———

GROUNDED

I SUCK IN A GLASS-SHARP BREATH, and I'm back on the orange couch.

The orange couch? I don't know an orange couch. I've never had an orange couch.

"Hey, I'm here," someone says soothingly. "I've got you."

I don't know that voice. Or do I? A thousand voices echo in my head, and I know it's one of them, but none of the names and times match together anymore. I'm a jigsaw puzzle with all the pieces shaken apart.

Shaking. I am shaking. I was shaking.

"The women took Ryan to the hospital," I mutter.

"Okay," someone says. "That makes sense."

That makes sense. Of course it does.

"They took him to the hospital, but he was dead on arrival."

I am shaking in a white-walled room. The hospital. No, Mom's office. Mrs. Evers called her with the news, couldn't bear to call me directly.

No, no, no, I'm on an orange couch. Mom's office doesn't have an orange couch. I inhale, and there's no smell of the dentist's antiseptic, no powdery latex stink. It's too warm for Indiana in October.

"Is it October?" I ask between rapid breaths.

"The twelfth," someone replies. Same someone. Calming voice. "A Tuesday, if that matters."

Prom was on Friday, so it can't be prom. I was at Mom's office on Saturday, so it can't be Mom's office. Tuesday was….

I'm walking down a street in Sycamore, talking to Ryan about our classes this semester. We reach an intersection, and I stop.

"Come on, Lil." He grins. "We're not in Dillsboro anymore. Veritable city-slickers don't wait for the walk signal."

He strides into the crosswalk with his hands in his pockets. When I don't follow him, he starts making chicken noises.

"You're such a dick." I jump into the intersection.

Someone leans on their horn.

"On Tuesday, I walked out in front of a sixteen-year-old getting their learner's permit," I reply automatically. "I wasn't trying to kill myself."

"Holy shit, Marce," someone says. "You did? Are you okay?"

I know that nickname. That belongs to… Heather. Who is that? She wasn't there on Tuesday.

"Not this Tuesday." I shake my head as I rock. I'm too hot and too cold. "Last Tuesday. A thousand Tuesdays ago. They sent me to the nurse, and a nice redhead named Dana came and asked me if I'd like to stay somewhere new for a while."

"Somewhere new," Heather says slowly. "Marcie, are you talking about when you were institutionalized?"

I don't like that word one bit. "Byrd. Call it Byrd when you're inside. It makes it easier to forget the bars on the windows." I laugh. "We're all birds in a cage."

"Okay, I'm going to put your hand on my ribcage, and I need you to breathe with me," Heather says.

Everything just happens to me when I'm a bird. I let her take my wrist. Her skin is warm under my hand. Up and down. Up and down.

"Like that," she says. "Just inhale, then exhale."

Inhale. Ryan is dead.

Exhale. Ryan is dead.

Inhale. I'm… not dead?

My next exhale comes out in a rush, and I force my eyes open, not sure when I closed them. Orange couch. Heather. My roommate for the last two years. It's been six years since that night. Five since the day in the crosswalk. I really didn't see the car.

"Hey," Heather says softly. "There you are."

My breathing is shaky, my face slick with snot and tears.

"Holy shit, I'm sorry." I straighten up away from her and scrub my sleeve over the whole mess. "I shouldn't have—"

"Shut up." She smiles. "I'm glad you weren't alone."

I blink a couple of times. She… really doesn't seem pissed. Or grossed out. Or anything like I expect. She's just smiling with a little worry in her eyes.

"Can I get you anything?" she asks.

"Tissue," I say thickly.

She obliges, and in her absence, I put a little more of my brain back together. The actual night. I haven't flashed back to that in years, and it's always the worst. Before it can catch me again, I shut her laptop.

"Fuck, sorry," she says as she returns with a whole box of tissues. "I hope this goes without saying, but I won't use that article."

I nod and accept the box then begin mopping at my face. My insides threaten to vibrate out of my skin. I'm back, kind of, but I'm fragile. I could fall back into my mind at any moment.

"Let me know if you need anything else. Seriously, anything." Heather sits back down. "Shit, I'm glad you're not dating Ben if Ryan stuff is still this bad."

Like a dog catching a scent, I'm suddenly single-minded. I know exactly what I need to keep me here and now.

I force a smile. "I'm just gonna get a little air."

Heather frowns. "Okay. Make sure you take your phone, and text me if something happens."

"Sure."

I don't spend nearly enough time cleaning myself up before shooting out the door, beelining for the *Arkly* offices. My heart hums to the simple beat of "*See-Ben, see-Ben.*" He knows how to escape his past. How to want to. He'll ground me for keeps.

As the sun sets, I walk up to the outside of the *Arkly* offices. A man leans against one wall, near the corner, smoking. I recognize him immediately by his eyebrows—perfect for scowling—and his drunken-professor clothes. That's got to be Scott. His mouth moves like he's talking to someone, but I don't see anyone else, and he doesn't have headphones in. My heart skips a beat. Am I imagining him? I veer out a little from the path, trying to see around the corner.

No one there. Well, except Scott, who puffs a neat smoke ring.

That's fine. I'm… not quite steady yet. It's just a tiny imagination, nothing to worry about. I cut back onto the path and head up the stairs.

Which means I'm probably also imagining the way Scott glares at me as I do. Just sane, normal-person imagining. I push open the door to the *Arkly*.

3 5

BETWEEN A ROCK AND A SOFT PLACE

Ben

"Yeah, I'll copy the flyer for you." I shoot Liam, one of the junior photographers, a smile and accept the single, neon advertisement for his band's underground show.

"Thanks, man." He claps me on the shoulder. "Printer credits are a bitch."

"Don't I know it." I smile one last time and twist away from him toward the copy room. I don't know anything about printer credits. My school didn't have them, and as an adult here, I don't even have access to those credits. But Liam's a nice guy. He doesn't need to know that.

As I walk, I check my phone. Still nothing from Marcie. I doubt there's anything wrong, but her suddenly calling me Theresa is unsettling. Hopefully, she'll text soon. I duck into the copy room.

Just in time to see some ridiculously tall emo guy sliding in through the window.

"What the fuck?" I look around, but I'm alone in here.

The emo guy's shirt catches on the sill and pulls up, exposing his

177

pale stomach and—my mouth goes dry—a fucking gun sticking out of his pants.

Current history was the hardest thing to learn when I woke up, but I'm not stupid. I know tall white guys in all black with guns mean I'm about to be on the news with the caption "first victim."

I hold up the flyer like it's a shield and back toward the door to shut it. "Is that real?"

He finally finishes slithering inside—fuck, he's tall too—and shoves black hair off his face. A lit cigarette dangles from his lips.

"What would you do if it was?"

I ease the door shut and lock it. "What would you do if I told you to get out?"

He snorts. "Make your fucking copies, news monkey."

With the door locked, I'm not exactly about to argue with the armed guy. I walk over to the copier and stick Liam's stupid flyer in. Somehow, I doubt he has a show to worry about after this.

The emo guy puffs on his cigarette, then glances back out the open window. I watch him from the corner of my eye. He's tall, but he's not strong. And I try to work out. I could tackle him while he's distracted, grab the gun, and—

He climbs back out the fucking window without a word. I blink. Someone tries the door, then rattles it when they find it locked. I blink again. Am I losing my fucking mind?

My phone goes off with a text from Marcie.

At your desk. Where are you?

Avoiding a school shooting, apparently. I scoop up Liam's copies, unlock the door, mumble an apology to Danny, and hurry to my desk. Maybe I should call someone, just let them know there's a weird asshole with a gun running around.

Marcie comes into view, her arms wrapped around herself and her face obviously tearstained.

"Hey, I'm here." I dump Liam's copies and wrap my arms around her. "What's up?"

"I saw—and it said—not *true*—"

She's on the verge of hyperventilating, and I don't know what to do, so I just sit in my chair and pull her into my lap. Marcie burrows into me. In fits and starts, the whole story comes out, and I realize she had a flashback.

An old pang of jealousy echoes through my chest. The doctors always said that's how my memories would start to come back. But I squash that immediately.

"So you came to me?" I wipe tears from her cheeks.

She nods. "I just… you said some stuff about, you know, not being the guy who fell off the cliff anymore, and I wanted to hear it. Again."

My chest warms. I never felt like this with any of my other girl-friends. Like someone important in their life, someone they needed to rely on. I squeeze her closer.

"You're not the person who watched him die," I whisper. "Or the one who walked into the road. Or the one who left that institution. You're Marcie, my… girlfriend."

My breath catches. We haven't exactly discussed exclusivity yet. But Marcie just crushes her mouth to mine.

"Thank you," she says. "That's exactly—"

My phone rings, and I grab it with a small frown.

Ah, fuck. It's 2:03, and Mom's calling because I forgot to call her.

"I'm so sorry, I have to take this." I cup Marcie's face. "I can meet you after. Bean and Gone?"

Marcie bites her lower lip. "I can be quiet. I just don't want to be alone."

I inhale slowly and nod, then pick up the call.

"Uh, hi, Mom," I say.

Marcie burrows her head in my neck. This is very weird. But I don't really want her to leave.

"Benjamin," Mom snaps. "I thought you said two PM was reliably good for you."

"I was just doing some work." I kiss Marcie softly on the top of the head. "Isn't that the point of these calls? To make sure I'm working?"

"Working and safe," Mom replies sharply. "And while it's lovely for you to know you're working, you're abandoning me to wonder when you don't call. I need you to pay attention to these things."

Marcie covers her mouth, and my stomach drops. She's shocked. She thinks Mom is awful. Then, her shoulders start shaking, and I realize she's laughing silently.

"Roger that, Sergeant Mom," I say to make Marcie laugh harder.

It works. Mom is less pleased.

"Did I raise you to talk like that?" she demands. "Certainly not. This college is doing things to you, things I'm not so sure I like."

"It's just a joke." I twirl a curl of Marcie's hair around one finger. "How are things?"

"Fine." She huffs a breath. "And you?"

"Well," I smile down at Marcie, "I'm actually seeing this girl I really like." She blushes prettily.

"I knew it!" Mom shouts into the phone. "Are you with her right now? Is that why you missed the call in the first place? Benjamin, I've told you, you don't have good judgment. She'll never understand you like I do."

"Uh-huh." I keep my eyes on Marcie, making sure she knows I don't care what Mom thinks without giving Mom any hints. "Maybe she's the bad influence you're talking about, not college."

"That's the first smart thing you've said this afternoon," she snaps. "You should break up with her immediately. She's just a harpy, waiting for a chance to take advantage of you."

I wink at Marcie. "I'll get right on that. Talk later, Mom."

And I hang up before she can say anything else. Marcie looks up at me with searching eyes, like she's trying to make sure I'm not seriously about to break up with the soft, sexy, and very upset woman in my lap. The last thing I ever want is for her to worry.

So I lean down and kiss her for all I'm worth.

36

RIVALRY

"Go, BABY, GO!" Heather shrieks from the stands next to me, her voice nearly swallowed up by the crowd.

I stomp my feet and cheer aimlessly. I lost track of Everett ages ago, but I can tell one of the boys in blue has the ball, and they're sprinting down the field, which I think is... good? Somehow, in the stands, the cold air stinging my face, wearing more bright blue than I could've sworn I owned before I started going to these games with Heather, I don't really care. Being here isn't about understanding the game beyond the scoreboard looming over the field, declaring it the final quarter, and the Ardent Alligators are losing to the Bennett Bears by three points.

It's about feeling alive.

The guy in blue throws himself into the end zone, and I scream my lungs out with everyone else around me. The game is ours! It doesn't matter if we make the kick. I don't even know how many points the kick is, but I grab Heather's arms and jump up and down with her as they line it up. The ball sails through the big, U-shaped bars, and the cheering on our side of the stadium triples in volume.

"ALL-I-GAT-ORS! ALL-I-GAT-ORS!" I chant with everyone else.

A dam I didn't know was holding us back breaks as the players finish exchanging handshakes.

"Where are we going?" I yell.

She grins. "To fucking party!"

My face hurts from smiling so much. Even without Ben here, it's so much easier to feel like myself, to ride the wave of the crowd down onto the field. We scoop up the team and pour out of the stadium, down Greek Row to the frat house Everett shares with at least half his teammates. I never let go of Heather's hand, and she never lets go of mine, not even when we find Everett, and he dips her into a dramatic kiss.

"I gotta change," he hollers over the noise as we reach the house.

"Marcie and I'll be on the dance floor," Heather replies.

I nod enthusiastically. Thudding bass already pours from speakers deeper inside the house, now a comfort through the soles of my shoes. A couple of guys who aren't on the team hang a banner—*Bears Bashed*—and another at their feet displays an equally cheesy slogan they would've used if we would've lost. I laugh. Win or lose, this house is going to be up all night drinking. There's something freeing about that.

Heather and I shed layers as we go, stuffing them into a beach tote she apparently brings to games where there's not going to be enough time to change in between. We transform from bundles of blue to actual college students. By the time we reach the dance floor, Heather wears a skimpy Ardent-blue crop top with a design of an alligator eating a bear that she painted herself and a pair of tiny, high-waisted shorts. Since Ben said he might show, she coaxed me into an outfit way outside my normal comfort zone: a T-shirt dress with the same design that hits me mid-thigh and a pair of fishnets. Apparently, my beat-up sneakers make the outfit grungy-cool. In the mirror, I felt like an idiot.

When I take my hair down and begin dancing with Heather, I feel like the person she saw. Easy. Effortless.

Songs pass. Heather dances like I'd never dream of being able to, like a girl in a music video. We share a red plastic cup I don't remember grabbing, and the room starts to go very slightly fuzzy around the edges. My ribs hurt from laughing, and my cheeks hurt from smiling. I throw my head back. I am so goddamn alive.

That douchebag who keeps slamming into me stands at the edge of the dance floor, talking to a couple of students. He leans against the wall with a cocky smirk, like everyone here belongs to him. Abruptly, it seems weird how often I've seen him around this semester.

"Do you know that guy?" I say in Heather's ear.

She glances over my shoulder then laughs. "I know we're really working on your social development this year, but I think alcohol is enough."

"What?"

Heather peers at me. "Oh, you actually don't know." She laughs like that's the funniest thing in the world. "That's Paper. Used to be a small-time dealer on campus. Weed, booze for freshmen. But this year, he's got some crazy new connection." She leans in like we're not sharing air, trying to hear over the music. "Don't tell anyone, but a couple of guys on the Alligators have been going to him for some steroid the usual tests can't pick up. Not Everett." She laughs again.

I join her, feeling as light and free as my hair around my shoulders. He's just some random drug dealer! I haven't touched anything harder than alcohol in my life—or at least, since my party phase, if I forgot—so it really is just a coincidence. The world is easy and beautiful. I have nothing to worry about.

Everett appears out of the crowd. "Mind if I cut in?"

I bow gallantly, and he crushes Heather to his body.

I don't know how much time has passed when someone slides an arm around my waist. I whip around, about to tell off whoever thinks they can just grab me, and stare up into Ben's blue eyes.

"Hell of a dress, Lancival," he says.

His smell enfolds me. My face warms. My whole body warms. I haven't seen Heather or Everett in ages, I'm a little tipsy, and my boyfriend is so goddamn sexy.

I flatten my back against him like I saw Heather do earlier and swing my hips in time to the music. He grips me, my T-shirt wrinkling under his hands. I grab him back and force him to match my pace. The thudding bass seems to slow to sticky molasses, sweet and sinful. I am officially having the perfect night.

Ben spins me around, keeping me close enough that I feel his cock start to stiffen, and kisses me. I gasp up into him. The music fades out as he swipes his tongue past my lips. We keep moving in rhythm with only each other. My whole body hums with want.

Someone taps me on the shoulder.

"Fuck off," I mumble against Ben's mouth.

Whoever it is taps again. I nip his lower lip, then whirl around, my eyes blazing.

"Can't you see—"

I meet Everett's far too sober gaze.

37

HOOK, LINE, SINKER

MARCIE

I OPEN and close my mouth a few times, grasping for an explanation. Everett knows exactly who Ben is, and there's no way he's not going to tell Heather.

"I need to talk to you," Everett says.

"No, you don't." I pry myself out of Ben's hold. "I'm, uh, drunk! Yeah, I'm drunk, and I don't know what I'm doing."

"Will you come upstairs with me?" Everett seems unmoved.

Ben steps in front of me. "Look, buddy—"

Everett towers up to his full height. Ben's no slouch, they're nearly at eye-level with each other, but all of Everett's muscles ripple under the flashing lights, a dangerous promise.

For a split second, I think I might just let them fight. Even knowing whatever Everett wants has nothing to do with romantic jealousy, the idea is kind of hot. Then, I shove myself between them, facing Ben.

"He doesn't want anything like that." I push up on my toes and kiss him, a testament to how much I might not be lying about the drunk thing. "I'll just… be right back."

Ben scowls. "If you're sure."

I nod and let Everett lead me away.

"That's not what it looked like," I say. "You don't have to tell Heather."

Everett blinks a few times. "Shit, Marcie, I'm not here to get you in trouble. I just have something you need to see before you go back to him."

Every hair on my body raises at the way he says that. "What is it?"

Everett shakes his head. "You've really gotta see it."

For the first time in the handful of parties I've attended here, I head up the stairs to where most of the frat brothers sleep. Couples doing way more than Ben and I were stud the hall, and moans escape from more than a few closed doors. Everett doesn't even glance at the debauchery around him. He just beelines for a room near the end of the hall and ushers me inside.

Predictably, the place is a mess. Clothes cover every surface, and most of them look dirty. A thick aura of cologne covers an equally thick stench of BO and alcohol. The twin bed along one wall isn't unmade so much as it has a loose comforter bunched in the middle. The only place untouched by the chaos is a wooden desk with a glowing laptop and monitor, and the chair sitting in front of it.

A chair which holds a wide-eyed Heather.

I whirl on Everett. "I thought you said you weren't getting me in trouble."

"In trouble?" Heather asks.

"I'm just doing what I think is right." Everett holds up his hands. "Give us a second, and I think you'll agree." He shuts the door behind me.

My hackles go up. "What is this, a fucking intervention? In the middle of a goddamn party?"

"Please, Marce, just listen," Heather says. "Haven't I earned, like, a second before you freak out?"

This is what she's been doing all along. Trying to get on my good side. Trying to make me prove that I'm crazy so she can send me back. But Everett is blocking the door, so I just cross my arms and turn to Heather.

"Give it your best shot," I snarl.

Heather stands. "A couple of weeks ago, Ben like, cornered me at work cause you didn't text him back."

I blink. "What? That doesn't sound like him."

"I wouldn't have expected it either." She shrugs. "But it gave me a really bad vibe. Like, stalker-y."

"You misinterpreted him," I say. "Ben's not aggressive."

Everett circles around me to Heather and rubs one of her shoulders. "I wasn't there, but I trust her interpretation. She navigates this place and tells me whenever one of my brothers actually crosses a line."

"That's different." I sound stubborn even to my own ears. "Is that it? He talked to you once, so you think I shouldn't date him?"

She bites her lip and looks at the floor. "No. After that, he started avoiding me, like, religiously. And pictures with you in the background started popping up in a lot of articles. So I… gave Everett that piece of glass."

I flinch back a step. "I told you to get rid of that. Fuck, you don't even believe me."

Heather meets my gaze. "I didn't."

What?

"I told her I needed a sample to compare to." Everett starts pulling something up on his computer. "It's not perfect, the blood is obviously degraded, but in theory, I'd be able to check if the DNA matched."

Heather pulls a gray beanie I've seen Ben wear a lot until recently from behind her back. "Hair was easier to get than blood."

I snatch the hat from her. "This is crazy."

"I know." She laughs helplessly. "I felt crazy. I just couldn't sleep if you got hurt, and I could've stopped it."

She doesn't seem like she's lying. I can't keep looking at her. I turn to Everett, who points at two sets of green lines.

"In theory, a pair of random people off the street shares less than 1 percent of their pairwise DNA," he says. "I ran the test three times because that was all I could get out of the blood. And, to be totally upfront, I'm a junior who snuck in to use the equipment. You're not exactly getting professional work. But"—he turns to look at me—"it looks to me like a 95 percent match. Maybe a little more or less."

The numbers bounce through my brain, unconnected. I am suddenly far away from my body, looking down at it from the outside. I don't look grungy-cool. I look very, very stupid.

"What does this mean?" someone says from my mouth.

"We don't exactly know." Everett sighs. "It's weird."

"Beyond weird." Heather nods. "The chances of this happening are astronomical. Unless the samples came from the same donor."

The same donor. Meaning that Ben and Ryan are the same person. *Could be* the same person.

I crash back into my body and begin laughing.

Heather and Everett exchange a look. She starts to step forward then steps back again.

"There are a couple of other possibilities," Everett says awkwardly. "Did Ryan have a twin?"

"Only child," I wheeze.

"And you guys were friends forever, so you'd know," she mutters.

I shake my head. "He moved to town when he was six. Maybe, instead of a drunk driver T-boning his dad, his dad actually took the other Ryan—Ben—to live in Illinois! And raised him to be evil!" That makes me laugh even harder. The room spins as I bend at the waist, and tears run down my cheeks.

"Maybe," Everett says doubtfully.

"And Ben is here to get revenge for his dead brother!" My stomach lurches because I'm laughing so hard. This is so goddamn funny. Just as soon as I finally start to get my life together, as soon as I think I might've found a way to move on, these two idiots burst in and try to rip it away from me! Just as soon as it's useful, I'm not crazy anymore!

"Was there anything else, like… weird about Ryan?" Heather asks.

"He thought mint ice cream tasted like toothpaste." More tears. I'm going to laugh up a lung at this point. "He hated Sondheim."

"Deeper than that." Heather's heels appear at the edge of my vision. "Closer to the twin thing."

"I don't know. He had a recurring nightmare about watching someone shoot his dad?"

My stomach lurches again, and nothing is funny anymore. Ryan made me swear on the treehouse we were going to build someday that I'd never tell anyone that. Or at least, that they were still happening after his mom freaked out and made him go to play-therapy for a couple months. The room spins. I spin. My skin is ice cold and burning hot. I'm so stupidly, ridiculously drunk.

Ben is Ryan. Ryan is Ben. And I bought his stupid amnesia story hook, line, and sinker.

I sprint to the bathroom to puke.

3 8

VOYEUR

BEN

I LEAN AGAINST A WALL, alternating between watching the stairs for Marcie, sipping some crap drink, and wishing I had a camera to capture this party. The frat guys converted a whole room of their house for dancing. There's no furniture in here but the DJ booth and a keg by the door to the kitchen. A hundred people in different shades of blue move never quite in unison, like a hive-mind that can't quite agree. I nod my head like I know the song and check the stairs again.

Still no Marcie. It feels like it's been ages, but I didn't check the time when she left. At least a little asking around got me the name of the musclehead who carted her off. Everett Beck. Apparently, he's Heather's boyfriend. Which could explain the "Theresa" call last week. Between what happened at the *Arkly* between us and how little we go over to Marcie's apartment, I can kind of tell Heather doesn't like our relationship. No idea why, but Marcie is probably upstairs getting lectured about how bad I am for her. I roll my eyes. Between her friends and my mom, we're verging on *Romeo and Juliet* territory.

I glance out the window next to me for something to do. None of the frat or sorority houses have huge yards, but this one has less than most because they took up most of it with the biggest hot tub I've ever seen. One of its walls intrudes on the thin sliver of grass I can see. A soaked bra flies through the air and catches in the branches of a nearby tree. I sip my drink and grimace.

Someone saunters past the hot tub to the tree. That emo guy from the copy room the other day! I twist so I can see out the window nearly perfectly, and if I'm right about the angles, can't be seen inside, then pull out my phone. If he starts shooting here, I can't imagine how much damage he'll do. I'd rather be the narc who broke up the party than dead.

A pretty, topless redhead joins him, and I grimace. Maybe I'm overreacting.

But instead of wrapping herself around him, she pulls a wad of soaked bills out of her shorts and offers it to him. He takes the money, barely glances at her body as he counts it. With a smirk, he reaches into one of the pockets of his cargo pants and pulls out a little bag of white powder. The redhead bounces in celebration, hugs him, then sprints away.

I put my phone away and turn back to the party. If he's a dealer, he's probably armed for professional reasons, and he doesn't want the army of drunk college kids here dead any more than I do.

Why the hell was he at the *Arkly*? If I didn't see him come in, I'd assume he was a confidential source, but he was in the office for all of about two minutes. I glance out the window again. Someone walks up to the dealer with their head low and their face shaded by a baseball cap. They're not even wearing blue, which makes them and the dealer basically the only two in a three-block radius wearing different colors.

The dealer's smirk fades as they talk. I watch a little less carefully. The only threat now is looking nosy, and everybody assumes journalists are nosy by nature. Finally, the stranger looks up enough that the strobes inside light his face.

My stomach drops. Scott's on drugs? I damn near plaster my face to the glass, trying to see what he's buying. Like I can tell the difference between drugs from a distance. Or without a labeled diagram. He seems so put together. I can't believe he has a problem.

The moment of truth. The dealer sticks his hand in his pocket. Now, Scott just has to provide the money, and I'll know how to talk to him on Monday. Or if I even should. He might just smoke weed and be used to his dealer.

The dealer puts out his hand first. He's holding—

Someone slams into me from behind, knocking me into the window and spilling my drink all over my shirt. Usually, I have a pretty good handle on my temper, but it flashes instantly out of my control.

"What the fuck do you think you're doing?" I shove up off the window and try to turn.

Two girls who don't look older than twenty giggle and bat their eyes at me. "We're sooo sorry. We were just dancing, you know, together, and we forgot to pay attention."

Lukewarm alcohol seeps through to my skin. "Do better next time."

"Totally." One of them smiles up at me. "Maybe you could help us? Come dance with us and make sure we're being safe?"

"I'd love to," I say sarcastically. "But unfortunately, being sticky isn't actually part of the babysitting description I signed up for."

"Just take the shirt off." The other one runs her hands up under it.

I jump back. These drunk children are flirting with me. They probably slammed into me on purpose, which doesn't do anything to help with my irritation.

"Go drink some coffee." I pluck her hand off me and shove them back into the blob of dancers a little less gently than I probably should. What the fuck am I going to do about my shirt?

Someone cheers outside, and I remember I was watching something. I turn back, but Scott and the dealer are both gone. Shit. Maybe… maybe I have no fucking clue what's going on here. And this party sucks a lot more than it did when Marcie was here. I'll talk to

Scott on Monday and try not to assume anything. For now, I need paper towels.

And to find Marcie. I don't give a fuck what Heather thinks of me. Marcie is too important to me to let anyone pull us apart, even some musclehead boyfriend.

3 9

WHO'S CRAZY NOW?

MARCIE

I WIPE my mouth and sit back from the grimy toilet in Everett's bathroom. Heather releases my hair. Everett dumps what looks like coffee out of a mug, rinses it, then offers me some water. Reluctantly, I accept.

Ben and Ryan are actually the same person. Might actually be the same person. This is the proof I was looking for, the proof that made me call Theresa and go through that box. Now that I have it….

My stomach clenches again, a tiny threat.

"How are you feeling?" Heather asks. "Did you just drink too much?"

This time, my laughter is dry and short. "'Just' is doing a lot of heavy lifting there."

She makes a small comforting noise.

"I gotta ask." Everett leans against the sink. "I saw you downstairs with him."

"Not a question," I say tiredly. I feel hollowed out. Ben, Ryan, Ben. Who can I trust?

"Are you seeing him?" Heather asks. "Did you have any dates from those apps?"

I've got nothing to lose. I lean my cheek against the tub to try to cool down. "I deleted them weeks ago. We've been dating since the night I gave you the glass."

"And fell asleep in the library." She sucks in a sharp breath. "So you're sleeping with him."

Tears bead in my eyes. I'm so stupid. "Do you really think they're the same person?"

"Yes," Heather says immediately.

Everett sighs. "I'm not so sure. It's definitely possible, scientifically. But, fuck, what's the point? What sort of person does this?"

I've been asking myself that question for weeks. Months, at this point. Almost nothing makes me feel crazier. I stare at a jet-black bottle of three-in-one soap and actually kind of wish for the days when I was just hallucinating Ryan. He was the person I remembered then. He didn't have any complex motivations or secrets I didn't already know. He was just my best friend.

"What do you know about Ben?" Heather says. "That article made the car accident seem pretty nasty. He wouldn't be able to come out of that without scars."

"He has scars," I mumble. "All over his head."

A beat of silence follows. I know what they're thinking. It's like watching them speedrun my whole relationship with Ben, except I don't think they're going to end up with four weeks of happiness.

"Did he say how he got them?" Everett asks delicately.

I pick my head up off the tub. "He did. Another big accident. Climbing, he said. But if there was an article about Ryan, there'd be something about him, right?"

"Depends on the size of the town." Heather shrugs.

"Tiny," I say. "Galesburg, Illinois. He climbed a local cliff with his dad, and they both fell. Other hikers found them. Only Ryan survived."

"Ben," Everett corrects."

"Ben, of course." I shake my head. "If there was an article, that would mean they were different people, right?"

"I guess," Heather says. "Baby, do you still have my credentials on your laptop?"

He nods. "I'll grab it."

My head spins. Wasn't I proving they were the same person, that I wasn't crazy? And now I'm desperate to prove they're different. The logic I relied on these past few weeks is turning to sand under my feet. I'm not crazy. I decided not to be crazy. Maybe Heather and Everett are the crazy ones now.

Everett returns with the laptop. Heather squeezes it onto her lap on the tiny bathroom floor and begins typing. Every now and again, she prompts me for details. When was my senior year? I'm sure he said Illinois? Do I know his dad's name? I answer to the best of my ability, my stomach roiling.

"I can't find anything," Heather says finally.

"That's not possible." I grab the laptop. She's on some kind of newspaper database, not one I'm familiar with, but research is research. I delete all her search terms, enter my own. Location, time frame, key words. Nothing comes up. I try again, a little different. Nothing. I broaden the search. Entries fill the page. I click through them one by one, my heart hammering.

"I can't find anything," I repeat.

I was right. I was wrong. I was so goddamn stupid. Hot tears streak down my face.

"Do you want me to go kick his ass?" Everett asks. "Because I'm happy to, conclusive or not."

I shake my head. I don't want him to hurt Ryan.

I nod. Ben needs to feel this.

I—

Whip back to the toilet and vomit again. Heather grabs my hair just in time. When alcohol and emotions stop tearing up my insides, I slump away from the bowl.

"I'm going to take you home," Heather says softly. "I think you need a little peace and quiet."

"Home good," I mumble. "Quiet bad."

"We'll watch some movies." I can hear the smile in her voice.

"I'll clear a path," Everett says.

I just want to curl into myself and stop thinking. Maybe forever.

Someone knocks on the door. Everett listens for a second then gestures for us to stay put. He heads out and closes the door most of the way.

"Apparently, his frat brothers have a code-knock for when it's one of them," Heather whispers.

I can't imagine anything mattering less right now. In the other room, the door opens.

"What's taking so long?" Ryan asks.

Ben asks.

Whoever asks.

Heather pales and takes my hand. I think about throwing up again, but I'm empty.

"Long talk," Everett says casually. "Ended in tears, you know girls. They're just cleaning up now."

"Let me see her," Ben-Ryan demands.

"Sorry, dude. When my girl wants privacy, she gets it."

"Well, your girl has my girl in there, and I'm pretty sure she's fucking up my relationship," he spits. "Let me in."

"No can do." Everett's voice is hard. "I'd suggest going back downstairs and waiting for Marcie there."

"Marcie!" Ben-Ryan yells. "Whatever they're saying, it's not true!"

I flinch back against Heather. There's a wild edge to his voice that I don't recognize.

"Uncool." The soft sound of flesh against flesh reaches the bathroom.

Heather mouths the word, "Shove."

They're fighting. Over me, in one sense of the word. I was so stupid to think this would be hot. The only thing hot is my feverish skin.

"What the fuck are you doing to her?" Ben-Ryan demands.

Another fleshy sound. Not like the last one. Maybe a punch?

"You don't want to fuck with me," Everett replies coolly.

"For Marcie?" Ben-Ryan laughs. "You have no idea what I'll do."

Nothing is hot. I'm ice cold.

"He's scaring me." Heather points to the window over the toilet. "If we climb out of that, we'll be able to get on a trellis and shimmy down to the ground."

More shouting outside. I don't think twice about my shaking hands, the droplets of alcohol remaining in my system. Heather's right. I'm terrified.

Together, we shimmy out the window, onto the groaning trellis. Only when the cold air whips across my face do I remember that Ryan had some behavioral problems in elementary school. Anger issues.

But Ryan made sure his temper never hurt anyone.

4 0

NEVER AGAIN

MARCIE

"THANKS FOR SQUEEZING ME IN." I smile tightly as I step into Dana's office the next day.

"It's no issue at all." Her answering smile is much more earnest. "I was planning on doing paperwork this weekend anyway. You've just given me an excuse to drive in and actually get done quickly."

I take my usual seat on the couch and fidget with the drawstring on my sweatpants. My head pounds, and I feel like death warmed over. Hangover breakfast wasn't nearly enough to pick me up after the night I had. Especially because I have to walk to Dana's office, and Ben-Ryan could be anywhere.

She pulls out her notebook and takes her regular seat across from me. I might be crazy—I definitely am crazy—but she almost looks excited to see me. Maybe she just knows I'm ready to stop lying to her.

"I went to the rivalry game last night," I start.

And the whole awful story tumbles out. She tuts when I admit I was drinking but doesn't say anything specific about my meds. She asks if this is the same Ben from my photography class. When I reach

Everett's blood analysis, her pen moves faster than I've ever seen before, like it's trying to outrun the words leaking from my lips.

"And then I went home," I finish lamely. "Heather and I stayed up basically until morning, made breakfast, and I'm here."

Dana sucks in a sharp breath. "That's quite a story, Marcie."

"It's not a story." My voice breaks. "I wish it was a story. But I have witnesses this time."

"Those witnesses being"—she turns back a page—"Heather Baxter and her boyfriend, Everett Beck?"

I nod.

"And you said they showed you proof? Physical proof?"

"Basically." I shake my head. A thin film of alcohol lays over my memories of the whole night, but I can picture Everett pointing to his screen, the green lines. "He showed me the little DNAs or whatever, but I wasn't looking too closely."

She nods, takes a few more notes. "Which brings us to the key question of all therapy: why?"

"They were protecting me?" I shrug. My stomach is starting to go to war with my breakfast again. I don't know if I can make it through this whole session without upchucking.

"No, Marcie, why would *he* do this?" she asks. "Do you have any idea? Do your friends?"

She sounds like Everett last night. What kind of a person would do this? My mind whirls.

"Revenge," I mumble.

Dana's posture abruptly changes, becomes soft in all the places it was hard a second ago. "We've talked about this. You didn't kill him."

Tears burn my eyes. "Apparently not!"

She hums, dismissing my response. "I mean that night. The person driving the car is responsible, not you."

I'm definitely going to puke if we keep talking about this. "Then I don't know!"

"I'm sure that's the hardest part." Dana meets my gaze and smiles softly. "Feeling like you were taken advantage of by someone you trusted. Have you talked to Ben about this?"

I shake my head furiously. "I've been avoiding him. We snuck out, and I took the back route here."

"Good." Dana looks back down at her notebook. "No matter what the truth is, you're undergoing a trauma. Taking care of yourself is the most important thing right now. Eat the things your body craves, sleep as much as you can. I can write you a note to get a few deadline extensions or absence forgiveness. And, of course, you'll never see Ben again."

"Never?" The idea shoots through my body like a physical pain, like I imagine being stabbed through the rib cage.

Dana raises her eyebrows. "I would say that's therapeutically advisable, yes."

"But... I have to ask him. Tell him. I don't know." I shake my head. Two sets of blue eyes merge into one in my mind, both of them painted with the hurt I last saw on Ryan's face. I can't walk away from him again.

"Tell him what?" Dana asks. "That your roommate's football-playing boyfriend thinks he might be your deceased best friend?"

My face burns. She doesn't throw how crazy I sound back at me like a weapon unless I'm on the verge of doing something really stupid, but it always hurts.

"Maybe?" I bite my nail.

Dana closes her notebook and looks at me seriously. "I wish you'd come to me earlier. We could've worked together, come up with a plan to step down your access to him slowly. As is, Marcie, I think you're in serious danger of triggering a total relapse. You're like an addict, and you've been using in secret. You're past the point where I can safely recommend anything other than quitting cold turkey."

I shiver. She really does seem worried. And I'm having a hard time keeping my thoughts in order enough to marshal an argument.

Fuck, I've been drinking again since Ben-Ryan came into my life too. Maybe Dana's addict metaphor isn't as off as it seems.

"Okay." I exhale slowly. "I'll just see him one last time to say good-bye, and—"

"No," Dana says with a softness that tells me she's starting to seriously doubt if I'm together enough to understand her. "Cold turkey means no further contact. I'm very worried for you, Marcie, and if you insist on seeing him, I'm afraid I'm going to have to call up the Byrd Institute and see if they have any space for you. You are on the verge of presenting a clear and present danger to yourself."

My stomach claws up my throat, all hot bile and grease. I'll do anything to keep from getting institutionalized. Even if it feels like someone reached inside that first stab wound and is rooting around through my organs.

"Cold turkey," I say numbly.

"I know we have a session Monday, but I'd like you to call me tomorrow so I can be certain you're all right." Dana scribbles down a few more notes and stands. "Okay?"

"Okay." I stand and stumble out of the building, the same overemotional, hungover zombie I stumbled in.

41

FALLING DOWN

BEN

WHEN THEY FIRST LET ME OUT of bed after my accident, I was starving for information. Mom told me all sorts of stories about myself, but there was a whole world to learn. And my ability to go to college in the fall hinged on how quickly I could re-learn it. So I told Mom I picked up a summer job and started people-watching.

In the morning, I would go to the nearest park and wait for someone interesting to walk by. Then, I'd follow them. Copy their walk. Listen to the conversations they had and fill in the blanks they left. Figure out their lives like the whole world was a puzzle, and if I placed enough of the pieces, the life I didn't remember would appear in shadow between them.

While I referred to it as people-watching, the old man who brought the case against me called it stalking. He dropped it when Mom explained. After that, she began teaching me the rules for seeming normal. I never meant anything by it, so I stopped people-watching right away. I haven't done it since then.

That is, until now.

I prowl along the campus sidewalk behind Everett and a trio of his meathead buddies. They make it easy to listen in, but they haven't talked about a goddamn thing worth listening to yet. It's just a wall of hangover complaints and play-by-plays of last night's game. Every now and again, they circle around to the topic of what actually happened at the party last night, and I perk my ears up. Then, inevitably, it circles away again. I didn't even know there were so many fratty euphemisms for throwing up.

Assholes.

I wish like hell I was home right now, nursing my own hangover and gearing up for the shoot I'm supposed to have this afternoon. But after a couple of Everett's fucking goons kicked me out of the party last night, after Marcie disappeared without so much as a text and my (very brief) stakeout of her place revealed the endless presence of Heather, I can't do anything else. I have to know what he did to her. Fuck, what *they* did to her. We were having too good of a time before they got involved for the answer to be anything else.

My mind drifts to Marcie last night. She looked like something out of a music video. Her hair caught every strobe and held it there. I should've taken a picture—a thousand pictures—but for the first time in my life, I wanted to touch her more than I wanted to hold a camera.

I think I finally understand why people kill. If Everett touched a hair on her goddamn head, I'd be perfectly happy to smash him and his meathead friends into a building with my fucking car. I clench my fists, crack my knuckles. They're too goddamn loud to hear me anyway.

"You fucking ghosted last night, dude," one of the other guys says.

I lean forward.

Everett laughs. "Did you see Heather? The fuck was I supposed to do, watch you limpdicks party?"

He sounds… fuck, I don't know. All the slang is right, based on how his goons are talking. But I can't see his fucking face, and I still don't really read tone from strangers well without their expressions. It's harder to relearn than one would think.

"Nah, but I saw that stacked brunette with her." Another one of the other guys smacks his lips. "You've been holding out on us."

This is it. He has to say something about Marcie now. I speed up, closing the distance between myself and them to a reckless point.

"Shithead." Everett punches the leering meathead. "She's—"

My phone starts ringing. Out loud. Because I couldn't risk missing Marcie's call. My pulse leaps, and I dart into an alley between two buildings before the guys I'm following can turn, then yank my phone out of my pocket. My stomach drops.

Not Marcie. Mom. And it's not one of our normal call times. I slam the "answer" button, already pissed.

"What?" I cradle the phone against my shoulder and peek out around the building. The meatheads are leaving. I probably already missed the main clue I might've gotten in four fucking hours of chasing these douchebags.

"Benny?"

She doesn't call me that unless she's really emotional. I haven't heard the old nickname since I left the hospital. My temper skips a beat.

"Yeah, I'm here." I lean back. "What's going on?"

"I'm sorry, Benny." Her voice sounds weak, fragile. "I know you live a busy life, but you're all I have."

The last of my anger dies. "Just tell me what's going on, Mom."

"I fell." She sniffles. "I was going down the stairs, and I just fell. Dr. Arroyo says I broke my collarbone and fractured a rib. She's testing me for osteoporosis."

My heart hammers. The whole world is falling down around me.

"I'm coming home," I say.

"No, Benny." She coughs, then groans. "I just wanted you to know—"

"Stop." I make my voice hard and certain, like Scott when the reporters start bitching. "I'm coming home. You need help, someone to manage the doctors and get stuff off high shelves."

"You're a good boy," she says softly. "You know I love you, right? Everything I've ever done, I did because I love you."

Another thing she almost never says. "I love you too, Mom. I'll be home soon."

I hang up. It's a fourteen-hour drive, so I need to pack up. And get some provisions. Maybe I can move her into some kind of home, or one of those senior neighborhoods, where someone would check in on her more often.

Loud, bro-y laughter splits the air, and I abruptly remember Marcie. Fuck. I've already missed my chance to hear what Everett had to say about her, and as much of a monster as I think he is, his reputation says he's dumb but nice. Certainly not the sort to brag about assaulting a woman in the middle of campus.

Footsteps sound at the mouth of the alley, and I flatten myself to the wall on old instincts.

"No, Arthur," someone snaps in a crisp, feminine voice, "you don't have time to *meet deadline*. It's unraveling now."

I peek briefly at the woman walking past. "Meet deadline" sounds like newspaper talk, and we do have a special rivalry-game edition hitting the presses tonight even though it's Sunday, but I don't know anyone at the *Arkly* named Arthur. I'm too slow. All I can see is blunt-cut red hair whipping past.

Forget her, Ben. You're just trying to distract yourself.

And I've got all the reason in the world to do it. I'm staring down the barrel of an impossible choice. Do I go to my lonely mom, the only person who sat by my side while I put myself back together, even if she's not always the kindest? Or do I chase whatever justice I can find for this girl I just met, but I really think I'm falling in love with? The picture I took of Marcie in class floats to the top of my mind. Beautiful and fearless.

A plan snaps together. I'll go home, pack up my car, and do the thing I've been avoiding since last night: confront Everett. Then, I'll tell whoever I need to what happened and go home to Mom.

The world might not fall down after all.

4 2

———

NOT GOING ALONE

Marcie

After therapy, I stand in front of my apartment door for a long moment. The *Arkly* is putting out a special paper tonight for the game, so Heather is at the office. Theresa told me a while ago that she splits Sundays between family time and grading, so I shouldn't call if I actually want to talk. Everett was really nice last night, but I can't exactly call him my friend. Which means as soon as I walk inside, I'll be alone.

With my thoughts. And the sinking feeling I can't just avoid this problem.

Something crashes on a lower floor, and I jump. It's a trash can lid. I memorized that sound ages ago. But right now, it feels like anything could be Ben-Ryan coming to get me. Maybe being alone isn't so bad after all. I shove my key into the lock and open the door quickly.

"Hey," Heather calls from the kitchen.

I blink. "Uh, hi?"

"Sorry, I was gonna text, but I literally just walked in." She pads out of the kitchen, still dressed for work and carrying a bag of chips.

"Scott closed the office early. Family emergency. We'll just put the rivalry special edition out on Tuesday."

"Good, good." I bob my head like a chicken, my hand still on the open door.

"Do you want to come in?" Heather asks with a small, worried smile.

"Oh, yeah, of course." I slam the door behind me and keep standing in the entryway, shoes on. With Heather here, the decision is made for me. I can't go talk to him. That's a good thing.

Right?

"So I pretty much exclusively talked about the DNA sample Ben-Ryan thing in therapy," I blurt. "And Dana—my therapist—was like, that really sucks, but hey at least you never have to see him again, and I didn't know what to say to that because the idea of never seeing him again makes me, you know, kinda want to pull my skin off?"

Heather sets her bag of chips down on the counter. "Shit."

"That pretty much sums it up." I do the same stupid nod. "So I was gonna sit here and decide whether to go talk to him until you got home, but, well... you're home."

She looks at me for a long moment. "Is saying 'don't go' going to change anything?"

No, my mind answers automatically.

I grimace, but the truth is undeniable. Coming home was just a stopgap. I have to see him. I have to ask.

"No, it won't," I whisper.

She sighs, brushes off her hands. "Just give me a second to change. I can't do this in a blazer. And I should call Everett for backup."

I furrow my eyebrows. "What?"

"Did you really think I was going to let you go alone?" she asks.

I FIDGET with the heavy-duty seat belt in Everett's open-door Jeep as we turn the corner onto Ben's street. The whole drive has been silent other than a thin stream of music out of the radio. Heather and

Everett sit in the front, holding hands. It's like we're riding to our deaths.

The door to Ben's apartment building opens, and he walks out with a cardboard box. He adds it to a couple others in the trunk of his car. He's moving out!

"Stop!" I say. "Park, whatever. He can't leave before I talk to him."

Everett slams on the brakes in the middle of the empty street, and I throw myself out of the car with Heather hot on my heels.

"Hey!" I yell. I should say his name. But what name? Who is he, really?

He turns anyway, and I watch his expression stumble through relief, elation, confusion, and anger. The final one brings me up short, a few feet away.

"Marcie." He smiles at me and holds out his arms. "I'm so happy to see you. I've been texting you all night."

I turned off my phone. I didn't want to speak to him after Dana agreed to the appointment. That seems so stupid now.

Ryan always smiled like that at the beginning of a new school year, like we didn't hang out all summer.

"And why the fuck have you been doing that?" Heather demands. "I think she made it pretty obvious she doesn't want to see you."

He scowls at her. "What's she doing here, Marcie? You don't need to listen to her."

I shake my head. I do. I don't. I have no idea. The world is going wavy, but no specific flashback is taking me, like there are too many with him right here in front of me. Why did I think I could do this? Why is he so angry?

"No, she needs to listen to the fucking facts." Heather stops beside me and crosses her arms. "I took your hat, by the way."

"What?" He starts to turn red with anger. "Are you fucking insane?"

I flinch. I am. She is. Maybe everyone is, at this point. Nothing will stay put. Only Ben gets so angry it distorts his face. Ryan's anger had a smaller canvas before he got it under control.

"Nope." She pops the 'p' viciously. "I'm dating a forensic scientist."

Everett flanks me on the other side. "She told you about her friend, right? And the crash?"

"You okay, Lil?" Ryan peers at me from under his disastrous seventh-grade haircut. "Theresa said—"

"Marcie, what the fuck are they talking about? Are you okay?" His face is painted with worry as he takes a step toward me, hands out like I'm a wild animal now.

Everett blocks me slightly, and Ben-Ryan stops.

"She got some things from that night, including a blood sample," Everett continues.

"Which is why we needed the hair to compare," Heather adds. "The DNA's a crazy match."

"We know who you are," Everett intones.

Ryan-Ben looks from them to me, his blue eyes wild. Neither of them have ever looked like that before. Feral-animal scared. Maybe he's the one backed into the corner, who needs to be handled gently.

"Marcie?" he says.

Finally, I find my tongue in my mouth. There's only one word worth saying.

"Ryan?"

His face drops.

A black SUV screeches around the corner.

43

WHAT THE FUCK?

BEN

Something in my chest reverberates when she says the name *Ryan*. Something else twangs when the SUV whips into the road. I don't know what to do with any of it, or the insane implication that a football player has been running forensic tests on me in secret.

None of that matters now.

"Get in the car!" I shout.

Marcie, Heather, and Everett just look from me to the SUV. One of its windows buzzes down, and something dark pokes out. Neurons I don't remember having fire. That's the muzzle of a gun.

No time left. I grab Marcie's upper arm—the meathead doesn't even try to stop me—and start yanking her toward my car. Theirs is across the street, and we need anything that'll stand in the way of us and bullets, even a crappy sedan. Marcie moves when I pull her like she was waiting for instructions. Heather and Everett spur into motion. I slam into the driver's seat, toss Marcie in the passenger's. The back door is still open when the first bullets fly.

In movies, bullets always sound so specific. In real life, they're just like a car backfiring next to your ear. That sound twangs in my chest too, even with the screaming in the car.

Marcie's screaming. Heather's screaming. Everett is just pulling the door shut, thank fucking God.

"Anybody shot?" I ask like that changes anything.

"Not yet," Everett replies.

I throw my car into gear as the people in the SUV fire again. The window next to me shatters, louder than any gunfire, but there's no pain. I peel off down the street, no destination in mind, in a hail of bullets like a goddamn action hero.

The back window shatters. Heather screams again as both of them duck.

"Still not shot," Everett calls.

All we can ask for at this point.

Marcie sits still and pale in the seat next to me, her hair braided back like always. She doesn't look at me. She doesn't look at anything. The only movement in her whole body is the trembling of her lower lip.

Fuck. I've ruined everything, and I don't even know how. All I can do now is channel hours of playing racing video games and hope that's enough.

I swing into a turn, wheels screeching. The SUV follows. I yank the wheel to the side just in time to dodge what looks like a tour group and curse.

"Take the back roads if you can," Everett says.

"Yeah, and I'll drift the fucking turns," I shout back. Now is not the time for helpful advice. It's the time for soothing his crying girlfriend and shutting the fuck up.

Still, I don't take the turn toward the quad. I head for the other off-campus apartments, half an idea in my brain. The SUV is keeping some distance, like maybe that's helping them line up their shots, but they are faster if they want to be. It's a new-model, and my vehicle is already wheezing.

"This can't be happening," Heather repeats over and over again.

That, I agree with. My stomach churns as I glance at Marcie again and realize she still hasn't moved. Things are very bad.

A bullet *pings* off the fucking plastic behind the back row of seats. No shit, Sherlock.

I whip into another turn and risk a glance in the rearview mirror. The SUV has a tinted windshield. I can't see anything but the gun now hanging out of the passenger's side window and the gloved hand holding it.

We skid around a final corner into the cul-de-sac of apartment buildings Marcie and Heather live on. Heather screams again. Marcie white-knuckles her hands in her lap. Everybody slides. Another thing that looks cool in the movies and just feels fucking stupid in a shit-colored sedan.

The SUV follows. Just like I guessed, they tuck the gun back inside and start closing the distance. They think we're cornered.

I take a deep breath. Fearless. Just like Marcie. "Hold on."

I gun for the narrow walkway between her apartment building and the next one. My car is a lot of things, but big isn't one of them. I measured it once. Just about as wide as two people walking past each other in opposite directions.

We bounced onto the paved sidewalk. The walls whip past, scraping my sideview mirrors. Chunks of plastic fly.

And then we're out on the other side, bouncing over a few little hills until we reach the road behind the buildings. No SUV behind us. I doubt they can see through that gap, much less drive through it. I slow down, but only a little. If they know this campus, they know the way to get here.

"Not the kind of back road I meant." Everett nods appreciatively.

"What the fuck?" Heather breathes.

Marcie still hasn't moved.

"Where do we go now?" I ask.

"Uh, my dad just bought this warehouse on the outside of town," Everett says. "Been condemned for ages. He's converting it to apartments. We could regroup, try to figure out what just happened? I'd love to know who shot at us."

"Nobody fucking cares who's shooting!" Heather screeches.

She's frayed. Pushed way beyond her ability to cope. Like we all should be. I glance at Marcie again, and a wave of panic threatens to swallow me. Why did I know that name?

Marcie reaches a hand back for Heather to hold. "You're absolutely right. What matters most is getting somewhere safe, and this warehouse sounds like our best bet." Her voice is soothing, but her face doesn't change. She's been pushed way too far.

By whom? Me? These two morons? Whoever the fuck pulled out a gun?

Why is the gun the least terrifying part of this to me?

"Hey, how did you know the SUV was trouble before the gun?" Everett asks. "We'd all be dead if you hadn't."

I don't know. It's like waking up in the hospital all over again. I don't know anything anymore.

For the first time since getting in the car, Marcie twists her head. She meets my gaze through the rearview mirror, a thin film of distance despite how easy it would be to look right at me. My heart pounds.

Her dark eyes are steady and certain as she looks at me.

I exhale slowly. Maybe the world is falling down. Maybe everything I know is wrong. And maybe, just maybe, none of that matters if Marcie can keep looking at me like that.

I ask Everett for directions and start driving.

4 4

RYAN

I FEEL like I'm in the eye of a storm as I stare around the abandoned warehouse on the outskirts of Sycamore. Everett is saying something about property values and what this place used to be, but I can't pay attention.

I've spent years falling apart at the slightest provocation. At a blond guy in the wrong place, at a cologne I haven't smelled since—

Ryan.

Who's walking next to Everett with his hands in his pockets, who I've fallen for every time I met him. I've spent years falling apart, and I don't know what it means, but right now, I've never felt more together. Heather sniffles next to me, clutching my hand. Everett seems to be babbling because he can't figure out anything else to do. But I'm not worried.

And I might not be crazy either.

"So, anyway, we could hit up the northeast quadrant?" Everett shrugs. "Heard my dad say something about a foreman or a surveyor or something starting over there. They might have some shit."

Ryan nods. I can't call him anything else now. He may have forgotten everything, but I didn't. And whatever danger is chasing us —him—he didn't create it.

"I also kind of have my whole life packed up in my car. My mom, uh, fell." He looks at his shoes. "I was headed to see her."

My stomach drops. "Beverly? Is she okay?"

He blinks, peers at me. "My mom's name is Laurel."

Heather crushes my hand in her grip. My stomach drops even lower. Why the hell wouldn't he have his real mom?

Or, the question I should've been asking all along, why would his real mom have lied to him?

A memory of two women pulling him out of the road bounces through my head. Is one of them this Laurel? But what the fuck would they want with him? Ryan's just a regular guy.

"Hey, let's just get set up," Everett says faux-pleasantly. "Once we're settled in, we'll all be a little happier."

I meet Ryan's gaze, and I know without asking that he's wondering a lot of the same things.

LUCKILY, SETTING UP OUR MAKESHIFT "CAMP" doesn't take long. Whoever Everett's dad had in here left behind a table and a few chairs in the northeast quadrant, which turns out to be a warren of offices. We drag the furniture into one office without any windows, supplement with Ryan's blankets and pillows that I definitely don't blush while setting up, and crack into what would've been his road trip snacks. It's about as nice as a hideout in an empty building could be, I think.

"So"—I grab a bottle of soda, hoping for energy—"what are we doing?"

Heather laughs a little wildly. Her hair fell out of her ponytail a while ago, making her look sloppy for the first time in as long as I've known her.

Everett smooths his hand over her shoulder. "Seems to me we

need to figure out who the hell they were actually shooting at and why then get enough proof to go to the cops."

I look at Ryan, waiting for his answer. Or just looking at him. He really did grow into his ears, just like his mom always said he would.

"Works for me." He shrugs. "I'll start with the biggest piece. I don't remember anything before my accident."

Everett and Heather gape. Heather actually stops freaking out for a second. I watch her reporter brain click back on, and the questions start flowing.

From there, it's easy. Ryan set the tone: there's no secret worth keeping. I talk about Dana, about Byrd, about Lily and Theresa. Heather explains all the digging she did, how there was a fire at the records office in Dillsboro a couple months after I moved, so she couldn't confirm Ryan's death certificate, how his mom seemed to drop off the Earth after she left town. Ryan tells us everything he remembers from those first few days after waking up, how normal everyone acted. He mentions seeing Scott with someone I recognize as that dickhead who keeps slamming into me, Paper, and neither Heather nor Everett seem pleased to hear his name come up. Everett walks us through the test he ran and what it actually means. Ryan lets him look over his scars, and I explain what I saw that night. When the room starts going wavy, I just look at Ryan.

He's here. He's alive. I didn't kill my best friend because I was too much of a coward to tell him I loved him.

Oh, fuck, do I love him?

"Maybe I'm out on a limb here," Heather says, "but it seems kind of coincidental that Scott keeps coming up, right?"

Ryan blinks. "What do you mean?"

"I know you're his class pet or whatever." She rolls her eyes. "But you caught him accepting something from a dealer who's been getting cocky lately, and he closed the *Arkly* early when we were supposed to be rush-printing a special edition. That's weird."

He frowns. "I guess, yeah."

"Maybe Heather and I take a look around the office?" Everett glances between Ryan and I. "Not to be a dick, but it seems like whatever's happening isn't exactly about us, and it'd be good to know if the Scott stuff is a fluke."

"No, we should—" Heather looks at me too. "I mean, yeah, we should."

"Yeah." My voice sounds strange, a little stilted. I finished the soda a thousand years ago, so it's worn off. Ryan suddenly being upset knocks the room on its head.

"Let's head, babe." The two of them leave. Heavy doors swing shut behind them, one resounding *thud* after another.

Silence fills the little office we've turned into our hideout. I glance at Ryan. He stares at his hands.

"Why did you come to Ardent?" I ask finally. It's the only question small enough to fit in my mouth.

He clears his throat. "No real reason? I'd been applying for a while, had a couple offers on the table. I was looking to get out of town, away from Mom. This one seemed… special."

Tears burn down my cheeks as I nod. "This was our dream school. We both got in, and we were going to go together. You for film, me for acting."

Ryan chokes out a laugh. "I don't know how to believe any of this."

"Me either." I stand. I have to do something, but I don't know what.

"I really don't remember." He looks up at me, and his blue eyes are full of a sadness so deep even I've never felt it before. "I'm sorry."

And I have the answer to my question. I sit in his lap on this stupid wooden chair in a warehouse in the middle of nowhere and wrap my arms around his neck.

"I love you," I say. "If I've learned anything from this, it's that I can't meet you without loving you."

His eyes are suspiciously wet too, but he puts his hands on my hips to steady me.

"Do you remember Lily?" I ask.

45

LILY

Ryan

My heart aches. That name echoes in my chest. "No."

Marcie swipes her tears away. "I think you do, somewhere in there, or you wouldn't have come to Ardent."

"I want to." I squeeze her hips, anchoring myself in her. "Tell me… something. About him."

"About you." She smiles softly. "When you moved to town in first grade, someone accidentally sent your mom the second-grade supply list, so you showed up on the first day with all this stuff other people didn't have. Markers and glue sticks and shit."

Another echo. Back in the hospital, right after I woke up, the doctors said things would feel familiar before I actually remembered them, but they never did. Was this what they meant all along?

"Your cubby was right above Theresa's," she continues.

"Theresa?" The word feels familiar on my tongue. "T?"

Marcie's eyes light up. "That's what we called her, yeah. Lil, Ry, and T."

They all sound familiar. No memories, but the unavoidable feeling

221

I know those names. I've said them all before. My gut clenches, and I can't keep doing this, but I don't want to stop.

I kiss Marcie—Lily?—and, as always, it's like a match to gasoline.

She wraps her arms around my neck and crushes herself against me. Here, like this, it doesn't matter who I am or who I was. There's just our bodies, moving in easy tandem. My hips rock up, and hers press back down. I flick my tongue against her lips, and she opens for me.

I draw in a breath through my nose, refusing to break the kiss. Her lavender deodorant fills my lungs like a punch to the gut.

"Lavender? Really?" Lily laughs and tosses her hair over her slim, preteen shoulder.

"Yes!" I say defensively. "It smells good, even with a dude's nose."

Another girl—T, I think—shakes her head. "We won't tell."

I believe them. I always do. And they always prove me right.

My first memory. The first real ray of light in the blackness of my past. Everything Lily said is true. And with her all around me, I have my first real chance to be a person instead of a thin skin wrapped around a black hole.

"Ryan?" She pulls back, caresses my cheek softly. Something wet smears.

Fuck, I'm crying.

I shake my head. "I love you too, Lily."

She smiles so wide it looks almost painful, and I can't resist kissing her again as I stand. She wraps her legs around my waist automatically. I carry her into the second room attached to this one, the room where we laid out all the pillows and blankets to make somewhere comfortable to sleep tonight, and set her down on them. She doesn't unwrap her legs, like she can't bear the idea of me getting any further away.

I wouldn't dream of moving.

I card my fingers through her hair, and another half-snippet of memory returns to me, a disastrous attempt by the two of them to teach me how to braid that resulted in a haircut for all three of us. She touches my head without flinching. Her fingers slide over the scars like they barely exist, like they don't matter now that we know we've found each other again.

Blood starts to drain below my waist. I need to explore every inch of her all over again, learn her knowing who she is, who I am. I release her hair and slide a hand up under her shirt. She arches up into my touch. When I cup her breast, I remember the awkwardness of the time I asked her why she was wearing two shirts because I'd spotted the strap of her first bra. I snicker against her mouth.

"What?" She smiles up at me, her lips kiss-swollen.

I used to dream about her. I justified them at the time, figuring it was just a puberty thing because we were so close, but I never dreamed about T.

"I'm starting to remember," I say softly. "We laughed a lot."

Tears gather in her eyes too. "Yeah, we did."

"We will." I tickle the left side of her ribs, where I suddenly know she's ticklish.

She squeals and twists away from me, laughing. God, she's beautiful. Even in sweats and a T-shirt, in an abandoned warehouse, maybe running for our lives, she makes my hand twitch for my camera. Maybe that's why I wanted to be a director, to capture her in motion. No memory of that flares to life, but I'm not worried anymore. I know they're in there. We'll find them someday.

Lily lunges up and tickles me in the back of my knee, where apparently I'm sensitive, and I dissolve into laughter with her. Clothes disappear as our fight continues. Both of our shirts. My pants. I pin her on her stomach and unclasp her bra. Things feel abruptly less funny when she sits up and lets the fabric fall away from her chest.

The dreams I had don't come close to reality. My cock aches with want. I dive forward, worship her skin until she's moaning loud enough to echo through the empty warehouse. She tastes like sweat and some vanilla lotion or something, tastes so perfectly mundane I know she's real.

Lily slides her hand down my chest and plucks the waistband of my underwear. "I don't suppose you packed a condom?"

I scramble off her, mourning the distance, and grab my pants. "No, but I've been keeping one in my wallet lately." I return to the warmth of her skin as quickly as possible, pluck the condom out, and show her.

"You're so smart." She kisses the tip of my nose.

An answer flies to my lips. "I wish I could show you a clip of this moment when we were studying for the geography final."

That calls another wide, wild smile to her mouth. Painfully happy. That feels right.

Before we can lose ourselves in emotions, I open the condom. Lily shimmies out of her underwear, then tugs mine off.

"So beautiful," I murmur as I slide the condom over my aching length.

"I love you, Ryan," she replies.

How long have I waited to hear those words?

"I love you too." I line myself up and sink into the wet heat of her.

We groan in unison. Lily locks her legs around my hips again, loose enough that I can still fuck her. I crush my lips back to hers and start moving slowly.

She tenses her legs, forcing me faster, deeper. I want to take my time, but her pace reminds me where we are. We found each other, sure, but in the middle of a hail of bullets that don't make sense with anything else either of us knows about me. We're stealing this moment from the jaws of some unknown, hungry enemy.

And I want to hear Lily scream my real name.

I pull back slowly, resisting her pressure, then slam into her and set a bruising pace. She sinks her teeth into my lower lip. I grab one of her bouncing breasts, twirl the nipple between two fingers. Her moans vibrate through my mouth. Way too quiet. So I release her lips and return to her neck, hungry for her.

She provides. Breathy moans turn into throaty ones, abortive curse words and mangled versions of my name. She surrounds me, so goddamn real and here. My balls tighten, a sure sign I'm close. But I need to hear her first.

I shove my hand between us, find her clit, and circle it in rhythm. My thrusts crush my hand against her in a way I'm worried might hurt, but it just seems to drive her moans higher, louder. Her inner walls squeeze, then start to flutter. I release her neck.

"Say my name," I murmur.

"Ryan!" she screams as she careens over the edge.

I groan, "Lily," and follow her the second after in a burst of pleasure.

When it's over, I kiss her softly and settle down to cuddle like I know she prefers. Condom trashed, panties for her, boxers for me. The world has never felt so perfect.

I take a deep breath. "Do you think—"

The door explodes open.

46

FEARLESS

Ryan

"Fuck!" I leap up, toss a T-shirt to Lily, and sprint for the door between this room and the one with the table and chairs, hoping to shut it. I don't have a plan past that. The reason we picked the second office is because it has no other entrances or exits, not even windows.

Someone fires a gun, and I throw myself to the side. The bullet thuds into something, and thank fuck, Lily doesn't scream. No matter what else I remember—or what I've recognized—I know immediately that my body isn't used to this. I wasn't secretly dodging bullets while everyone else was in eighth grade. Which means I've pretty much got Ben's skills to rely on.

We're fucked.

"Present yourselves, and we'll handle this cleanly," a feminine voice says.

"Dana?" Lily whispers.

I glance at her. She's put my T-shirt on, but it barely reaches mid-thigh on her. And she looks completely lost. So am I. I don't know anyone named Dana, or—

No, I kind of know that voice. I heard it once. My skin goes cold as I place it with the woman walking past me earlier.

Dana fires another bullet, seemingly into the ceiling this time. "Come the fuck out here. Now!"

I hold my hand up at Lily. If there's one skill Ben had to rely on, it was lying. Maybe I can do it well enough to buy her a second. She crouches on the blankets, ready but not moving. I step into the doorway.

A woman with a red bob and Scott, both wearing dark suits and holding handguns, stare at me.

"We know she's in there." The redhead, Dana, points her gun at me. "We need both of you."

"She left with Everett and Heather. They think I'm lying about my memory." I hold my hands up and look only at Scott. We've seen each other every day for months. That has to mean something. "What's this about?"

"You put your foot in it, kid." Scott shakes his head. "Again. So I'm here to make sure the wife doesn't go soft again."

Pieces click into places as hurt rips through my chest. Things Lily knows, things I've seen. Both of them wear wedding bands, glinting at the grips of their guns, but Scott never had any pictures. And Lily saw two women drag me away. Did I get too close to something last time, and that was why they hit me?

Did Scott ever think I was any good?

"Marcie," Dana singsongs. "Come on out, and we can handle this like adults."

The way she speaks abruptly reminds me of Morgengraun, the cheesy witch in *Manticore Quest*. I push the thought away, looking for something actually useful. There's one blanket in this room, a couple half-finished sodas and bags of chips, and the door out behind them.

When Lancival first finds Morgengraun, about to lower Gwendivere into the cauldron, he realizes he just needs to distract her. Then, the final level is mostly a chase sequence through the level before it, but backward. Maybe this is fucking stupid, but I don't have anything else. And I know just how to warn Lily.

"She left," I repeat as I reach for a bag of especially powdery, cheesy chips. "Just like Lancival in *MQ*."

"What?" Dana says.

At the same moment, Scott barks, "Stop moving!"

But he's too late. I grab the bag and fling the chips in an arc. Since they're holding their guns with both hands, they each get a face-full of cheese powder and start coughing. Like clockwork, Lily sprints out of the room. I reach the splintered door out a second before her.

"Nice plan." She grins at me. "Lose 'em?"

Scott roars and starts fumbling around inside. I know what I have to do. Dana got a little more cheese. I shove Lily in one direction, put a finger to my lips, then turn the other way.

She yanks me back in for a split-second kiss. "Don't die again."

I smile. "I'll do my best."

She sprints away silently. I run as loud as I can in the opposite direction just as Scott bursts out.

For effect, I yell, "Fuck!"

His heavy footsteps follow me. A bullet wings through the hallway and shatters a glass window in one of the doors.

"I fucking told them," Scott shouts. "Kids just make a mess of things."

Them?

I can't let him distract me. My lungs are already burning a little, and the faster I run, the harder it is to forget that I have nothing between me and his gun but cotton boxers. I whip through turns as fast as I find them, thanking Everett's dad for buying such an insane building.

"But no, Marissa was *made* to be a mother," he rants. "Sean just wouldn't have a full life."

Those names echo in my chest, but vaguely. Like they're from a long time ago. Another turn, and another. Bullets fly. I zig and zag across the narrow hall.

"Fucking morons." Scott sounds disgusted. "I told them nothing was more important than our work."

One last turn, and I come up short. Dead end. Nothing but a single door. Which means I have no choice but to yank it open, run inside, and hope.

Just like most of the offices, it's nearly completely empty. One filing cabinet. A set of blinds so cobwebbed I don't want to touch them. I duck behind the filing cabinet. A jut of rusted metal pokes out of the side, and I snap it off. I don't know how to use a knife, and the jagged edge cuts my palm, but even a shit weapon steadies me a little.

Not a lot. My hands shake. Jesus Christ, I'm so fucking scared. Scott follows me inside.

"This isn't fun for me, kid." He fires into the side of the filing cabinet. "Just let me put a bullet in your brain, nice and clean. Won't even hurt, unless you make me shoot around this hunk of junk."

I jump. "Why are you doing this, Scott?"

He laughs. "At this point, call me Arthur."

Another long-ago echo, and something else. A memory.

I stare up into blackness. There's something there, I know. A monster in the night.

"Please." I know I'm speaking, but my voice is higher than I've ever heard it. "Please, don't."

My heart hammers in my throat. I want to fight, but I can't see the monster, and it's so much bigger than me. I'm so small. It laughs, low and rumbling.

There! A shape in all black against the darkness. The monster moves, and its claws glint in light I can't see.

"Don't shoot my dad," I sob. "Please, Arthur!"

I stand up slowly from behind the cabinet.

"Thanks, kid." Scott—Arthur trains his gun on me. "I'd hate to fuck this up again."

"You killed my father," I say.

He blinks. "Marissa said you hadn't had that dream since the accident."

That's damn near as good as confirmation. I clutch the metal in my palm. "Why?"

"He found out. Wanted to turn all three of us in." Arthur shakes his head, hefts his gun. "I don't owe you an explanation. Hold still while I finish this."

A fuzzy memory of a blond man with a kind smile floats through my mind. My dad.

For him, for Lily, I can be fearless.

I throw myself out from behind the cabinet, trying to go low, just as Arthur pulls the trigger. Pain screams across the left side of my chest. Good thing I'm right-handed. I hit Arthur hard in the chest, yell with how much it hurts and the anger bubbling in my veins. We land in a pile, and I don't hesitate. The jut of metal lodges deep in his throat, and red blood leaks around my fingers.

"You… little shit," he wheezes. "Should've… smothered…"

Arthur goes still. Pain roars through me. I slump off him, to the floor, and the world turns gray.

47

STARING CRAZY IN THE FACE

Marcie

I sprint down one of the identical halls of this part of the warehouse, Ryan's T-shirt whipping around my otherwise naked body, my heart hammering in my throat.

Being shot at from an SUV was crazy. Finding Ryan was crazy. The shooters following us to this warehouse is crazy. But one of the shooters, one of the people who tried to kill Ryan in the first place, being the therapist I've trusted with my life nearly every day of the past six years?

I'm starting to think I don't actually know what the word crazy means anymore.

Scott thunders after Ryan, and I pray he's got more of a plan than running and hiding. The "newspaper editor" looks furious.

Oh, fuck, did he kill Mrs. Mathers?

Heels click along the hallway behind me, and I put all thoughts of the ex-editor out of my mind. Apparently, my bare feet aren't quiet enough. Dana—if that's actually her name—is coming after me.

I blink, and I'm in that crappy little park on prom night, watching two women drag Ryan away. Was she really one of them? How could I have seen her for six years and never noticed? Maybe that's what makes me crazy.

I blink again, and I'm back, running. It's like a dream. Every single hallway looks like the next, and I swear to God those heels are always getting louder. Or coming from a new direction. Surrounding me. There is no escape.

Maybe she's not shooting because she's going to send me back to Byrd. It's not like they wouldn't take me with the story I've got to tell. My stomach churns, and I skid around a corner.

Dana's there, at the end of the hallway. She smiles like she always used to.

"When Arthur suggested I go to you in that hospital, I almost ripped his head off," she says pleasantly. "You were no loose end worth worrying about. You didn't have the guts. But he insisted."

I scramble back, and my hand lands on a doorknob. I yank it open.

"Run if you like," Dana calls. "I'm thrilled Arthur suggested it because now there's nothing you can do that will surprise me. I've been keeping an eye on Everett since you became friends with Heather. I know the plans to this building like the back of my hand."

Just an empty room, somebody's old office. There are rings from coffee mugs on the floor, like someone kept working here long after they took all the furniture out.

"But you didn't know I was seeing Ryan." I back into the office anyway. It's not like I can go toward her.

She frowns. "The lying is new, I'll admit. I thought you were better behaved than that."

My back hits a wall. There's nowhere else to go. I'm going to die, just as surely as if I'd actually walked in front of that car all those years ago.

Dana raises her gun. "I should've made sure Ryan was dead the first time, but Marissa was always a softie." She laughs. "Beverly, I guess you'd call her."

My stomach drops to my toes. "What?"

"Hadn't you figured it out?" She laughs. "Hon, who else did you think would pull his sorry ass out of the road?"

I shake my head. "Ryan's mom loved him."

"Not enough." She puts her finger on the trigger.

When Ryan died, I lost everything. With Ben, I thought I was getting it back. But that just means I need Ryan in my life to be whole. And I love him, but I have to be a whole person on my own. I can't be his best friend, or Heather's roommate, or the crazy girl my whole life.

I have to figure out how to be Lily. And to do that, I have to live.

Dana fires. I drop faster than I've ever dropped before and hit the dusty ground. Plaster shatters and rains down on my head. I've never fought anyone, never even held a gun, but I've got six years of studying how the human body works. That has to mean something.

She shoots again, I scramble, and the tile next to me sprays up in gray-blue shards. My stomach churns. I don't have another choice. I palm a jagged shard and turn.

Dana is already closing the distance between us, staring down at me, her eyes cold and mocking. "You were always so goddamn worried you were crazy. You want to know a secret?" She leans in, presses her gun to the center of my forehead. My blood runs cold. "I didn't even have to suggest that. You were so goddamn crazy you made my job a breeze."

I start to fall into myself, but then I hear Ryan's voice in my head. Grown-up Ryan. The real one.

She tried to kill a teenage boy. We don't even know why! Who the hell cares what she calls crazy?

He's absolutely right. And I'm not the crazy girl anymore, even if I'll be crazy for the rest of my life after this. I look up slowly, along the leg of her charcoal pantsuit, and find the spot I'm searching for. Just above her knee, on the inside of her leg. This has to work. I adjust the tile shard and slice.

Dana flinches back, then laughs. "That's it? That's your last stand? I've got a gun to your head!"

Blood spurts out of the slice in her femoral artery, wide enough that it can't clot quickly. With an injury that size, she'll bleed out in five minutes. Her hold on that gun to my head weakens, and horror crashes through my veins. I had no other choice. But now, Dana is going to die. I killed her.

"What the fuck?" She tries to swing the gun back up as weakness claws at her limbs.

She still has just long enough to try to take me with her. I surge up, hoping she's weak enough, and hit the gun. Pain shouts across my knuckles, but the gun drops from her hand. I kick it further away.

"I'm sorry." I wince as I push her.

She crumples to the tile, unable to resist. I start to walk away.

"No!" Dana screams. "Get back here, Marcie, I'm—"

"Lily," I say.

Somewhere else in the warehouse, Ryan yells.

48

LAST CHANCE

IF I THOUGHT RUNNING through this warehouse was torture with Dana chasing me, I was an idiot.

"Ryan!" I scream.

Still no answer. I retrace my steps back to our little hideout, take off in the same direction he did. My heart hammers. Is he hurt? Should I have taken the gun? Am I going to round the next corner and come face-to-face with Scott—Arthur? Am I already too late?

I pour on whatever speed I have left, looking for any clue.

There! That stupid cheese dust Ryan threw at them, smeared on the wall. I hang a sharp right.

"Ryan!" I shout again.

Nothing. With each step, I feel like I'm falling through time. The park on prom night. The car before his funeral, when I refused to go. The street I almost followed the hallucination into. The time I got lost on a field trip, and he was the only one to come looking for me. *Ryan, Ryan, Ryan.*

I am not going to lose him again.

The smell of iron pulls me to an open office. I whip inside and skid in a puddle of blood.

Blood spatters like it never does in movies, in every direction, hot and red and tasting like iron.

No! I'm here. I'm saving him. I'm a goddamn nurse, aren't I?

My training snaps into place, and I approach the pile of bodies in the middle of the office floor. Ryan is on top. As gently as I can, wishing for straps or a gurney, I roll him off Arthur.

Good news, the jagged metal in Arthur's neck is probably responsible for most of the blood. Bad news, Ryan's been shot on his left side, in a spot that could easily be heart or lungs or nothing particularly deadly.

Focus, Lily! RPM!

R is for respiration. I put a hand on Ryan's chest and pray.

The faintest ghost of pressure raises my hand. He's breathing! Not as much or as well as I'd like, but some. It's not over yet.

I have to stem the bleeding before I check anything else. I yank Ryan's shirt off over my head, wad it up, and press the ball onto the entry wound. More blood oozes onto the floor. Fuck! I slide my hand under his body, carefully, and discover the spatter of blood I saw on his back wasn't Arthur's but an exit wound. There's no bullet to remove, but only blocking one side won't stem the bleeding. I rip Arthur's shirt off his body without checking to see if he's alive, wedge it under Ryan, and press down with all my weight. Then, I push my mouth against his and exhale air into his lungs, feeling and listening for it escaping out his side.

No sign. Not a sucking chest wound. Fuck, his lungs might even be okay.

Back to the checks. P is for perfusion. I take one of Ryan's fingers and squeeze the tip. The color returns far too slowly. He's already lost a lot of blood. I need my phone, but my phone's all the way back where we started, and there's no time. M is for mental status, and I don't even have to check that. He's unconscious. He's bleeding out, just like Dana on the other side of the warehouse. I lean on him harder, trying to force all the blood he has back inside his body.

"Please," I whisper. "You've survived so much. You're a miracle already. Don't let something as stupid as a bullet take you down."

I lean down and kiss him this time. There's nothing in any of my textbooks that calls for this, but in my textbooks, this is a conflict of interest, and there's nowhere else in the world I'd be right now.

He coughs against my mouth. Hot blood spatters on my lips. I yank back and stare down at him.

His eyes flutter open. "Lil?"

"Shh." I can't keep the smile off my face. He's awake. That's an amazing sign. "Just relax."

"I feel—"

"Shush." I put a finger to his lips. "We'll talk later."

"Lovoo," he mutters against my finger.

"I love you too." I grin.

"Marcie?" Heather yells. "Ben?"

"In here!" I scream. "Call 911!"

Footsteps pound down the hall toward us. Minutes later, Everett and Heather arrive. Everett, with his phone against his ear, immediately wheels back out as he realizes I'm naked. Heather hurries in, pulls off her jacket, and wraps it around me.

"The SUV is outside," she whispers.

"They're dead." The words tear from my lips. "Scott and my therapist."

Everett joins us. "Ambulance is on its way. Anything I can do?"

"Pressure." I trade off our weights on Ryan's makeshift bandage slowly, without ever letting up. My hands are shaking. "Don't relax for a second."

Everett nods.

Heather stares at Arthur, whom she knew as Scott. "We found all this shit, but...." She shakes her head. "Apparently, he's a fucking federal agent. FBI. And he's been working with Paper to get him better stuff in exchange for a cut of the profits. He has a wife named Julia, is she...?"

"Dana," I say grimly. "Sent here when I said I was seeing Ben to keep an eye on me."

Heather sucks in a breath. "Jesus fuck."

I nod, but it's hard to think about anything other than Ryan on the floor. The ambulance isn't getting here fast enough. He's going to die—again.

Heather takes my hand. "You're not going to lose him. Or any of us."

I glance at her. "Reading my mind?"

"That's what friends do." She smiles tiredly. "At least I'll have a hell of a scoop for whenever *The Arkly* reopens."

That coaxes an exhausted laugh from my lips just as I hear the first siren.

Everything begins happening very quickly. EMTs pour into the room, check Ryan quickly, then load him onto a gurney with my makeshift dressings still intact. Heather disappears to get me actual clothes, and I change in another office with the door cracked so I never lose sight of him. I load into the ambulance with him. A blood-stained Heather and Everett wave us off.

The hospital is blindingly white. I sit in the waiting room for hours while Ryan is in surgery. I call Theresa and tell her what's happened. She threatens to drop everything and fly out, but Jackson reminds her she has the Thanksgiving play that night. I tell her I'll keep her updated. I don't know how I could do anything else. My heart is beating beyond the swinging surgery doors in time with his.

Finally, they lead me into a room. There's a bed, but none of the nurses will tell me what's going on. Is he alive? Is he dead?

A nurse pushes a gurney with an aggressively bandaged Ryan into the room, transfers him to the bed, and leaves. I nearly burst into tears. I think I would, if I had any liquid left in my body.

"Lil?" he mumbles through cracked lips.

"Here." I take his hand. "I'm never gonna be anywhere else again."

4 9

COMING HOME

RYAN

THE DAY after they release me from the hospital, I drum my fingers on my knees as the suburban streets I thought I knew all my life but really only knew for six years whip by outside. Heather and Everett dug up nearly everything I could want to know about Julia and Arthur Daugherty but much less about their apparent partner, Marissa McGuire. Or Beverly Evers. Or Laurel Andrews. My mother.

Lily puts her hand on mine. "Stop fidgeting. If you mess up your stitches, they're going to kill me."

I smile. "Kill you? Why? I thought your quick thinking saved my life?"

She shakes her head. "It was a through-and-through, and it only got your large intestine. Painful, likely to get infected, but not immediately deadly."

"We waited their ten days!" I tap my other fingers on my other knee, even though it makes the recently stitched surgical scar in my side burn.

"I am driving." She scowls at me quickly. "Do you want to not die in another car crash, just to prove that you're immortal?"

"Sorry!" My smile strains as I hold up my hands and the stitches shout.

"What are you going to say to her?" she asks.

I blink. "No clue."

The day after I woke up in the hospital, I called Mom. My real mom. The one who was in the car that hit me and hid my identity from me for six goddamn years. I told her, very simply, that Arthur and Julia were dead, and that in ten days, I'd be coming to see her. She got very quiet, then just said, *"Okay."*

"To be honest, I don't know if she's even gonna be there." But a strange part of me is really hoping she is.

"Time to find out." Lily pulls into the driveway, parks, and takes my hand. "You ready?"

Her dark eyes on mine are exactly what I want to be: fearless. So I nod and climb painfully out of the car.

I remembered the house I lived in while I knew Lily a couple of days ago. It makes this place look like a stranger's house. But I still know that you have to press the doorbell, release, then press it again if you actually want it to make a noise.

A moment later, Mom opens the door. She looks tired and—I notice with a flare of temper—uninjured.

"I see the fall was a ruse," I say.

"Most of it was." She looks at me, then Lily. "Do you want to come in? Or should I get one of my guns from storage, and you can just end this on the lawn?"

Disgust sears into the place where my anger was. "I'm not going to kill you. That's your way of handling problems, remember?"

She steps back and holds the door open wordlessly. Lily looks at me, silently offering a final out. We can get in the car and drive away right now. I shake my head and follow my mom inside. I have to know.

"Coffee?" she asks. "Lily, am I remembering you drink Darjeeling?"

"Stop pretending, Mom." I close the door behind me and cross my arms. "I want to know everything."

"Forgive me for trying to be pleasant." Her voice verges on the coldness I've known for the last six years, a tone I never remember hearing as Ryan. But she seems to snap herself out of it. "Fine. At least sit in the living room with me."

I follow her into the sparsely decorated living room. Lily takes the couch, Mom the armchair. I stay standing.

"Dad," I say.

She winces. "Do we have to start there?"

"Is, '*Why did you hit me with a car* better?'" I snap.

She looks up at me, and tears fill her eyes. "I'd like to start by saying how sorry I am."

I breathe in, hold it, and release it like Lily taught me to stave off the feeling I might actually kill my mom.

"Dad," I repeat.

"Arthur and Julia were friends," she says. "Back when all four of us worked in the Bureau."

My eyebrows jump. I didn't see that coming.

"Sean"—she grabs a tissue as her tears start to spill—"your father wanted a big family. So did I, but we didn't make enough, not to live in D.C. So when Julia offered me a money-making opportunity on the side, I took it."

"And that was the Russians," I say. Heather and Everett found evidence back through their whole careers of Arthur and Julia working with the Russian mafia. Paper was just the latest in a long line.

She nods. "I tried to get out, but they said they'd kill me. So I kept my head down. But your father, he was the best man I ever met. You remind me of him." She offers me a teary smile. "And he knew something was wrong. So he looked and looked until he found out what the three of us were doing." She stares at her hands. "I told them I could handle it. Instead, he talked me around. We could come clean, turn the two of them in, and start again."

My stomach churns. I think I know what's coming next.

"The next day, Arthur killed him in front of you," she says. "You were five years old. The Bureau offered me a pension and a Witness Protection placement in Indiana."

"The dreams," Lily says wonderingly.

"Memories." Mom starts shredding her tissue. "Ones I made the mistake of mentioning to Julia when they started recurring."

"Right before prom." Realization dawns. "For the first time in ages, I started having them at the end of senior year. I thought they were just stress dreams."

"You'd seen Arthur in town," she says. "Or at least, that's the theory. He was passing through to… pay me."

"You were still working with them?" I sink to the couch in disgust. Lily pats my knee.

"I had to!" Mom leans forward, her eyes wild. "If I didn't—"

"They'd have killed me?" I ask flatly.

She looks away again. "Julia told me we were just going for a drive that night. She wanted to see you all grown up. And after… they wanted to place you with a stranger. I'd rather be theirs for the rest of my life than let them do that." She swallows. "I don't ever expect you to understand. They're the worst regrets of my life. But I do love you, and I am sorry."

I take a long, deep breath and look at her. "I don't have anything to say to you."

I grab Lily's hand, and we march out of the house. For a moment, I feel triumphant.

The next day, I drag us back to the house. Something isn't sitting right. I want to be a whole new person, put this behind me and forget it ever happened, but I can't. Especially with Lily sleeping beside me, I can't ignore the past.

Mom opens the door. "I thought you didn't have anything to say to me?"

"I don't." I push inside. "But you have more to say. I don't want the summary anymore."

We sit on the couch again, and when Mom joins us, she looks a little bit hopeful.

EVERY DAY FOR A WEEK, I go over and listen to her talk. At first, her stories make me angrier than I've ever been before. Even the nice ones about Dad. She doesn't deserve those memories for what she did to him. But, slowly, I start to see what she means when she says she had no choice. Lily tells me more about Dana, the careful ways she applied pressure. Arthur knew how to make her feel special, just like Scott did with me, and then how to rip it all away. After what happened with Dad, Mom was alone. She couldn't tell anyone without jeopardizing my safety.

On Sunday, I agree to have dinner. Lily and I dress up, bring a bottle of wine. Mom cooks. And when we're done eating, I look at her.

"I don't forgive you," I say. "I don't know if I ever can. But…" I sigh, "I've spent too long without a past already. So maybe we can keep talking."

Mom's smile is tight. "I'd like that."

5 0

WHERE IT STARTED

Lily

At the end of our two weeks with Ryan's mom, I'm lying in the bed in our hotel room waiting for him. I'm completely exhausted. Since he's been going over there almost every day, I've been amusing myself with what there is to do around Galesburg, and there's really not a lot. I'm bored enough that being bored makes me tired, but we're finally leaving tomorrow. Heading back to Ardent, because I still have a lease, though we haven't really talked about what happens next for us.

I guess I could've kept going to his mom's house, but watching the two of them reunite has been… weird. I just keep thinking about my mom, whom I cut off with everyone else. She didn't even kill my dad via choices she might've been manipulated into making. I've picked up my phone half a dozen times, intending to text her and see how things are. But I don't know what follows that. I can't imagine going back to Dillsboro for the holidays, reappearing at family gatherings like nothing happened. It just kind of feels like there's the person who belonged there—and then there's me.

But maybe I'm being selfish. Theresa keeps demanding I visit, and

I can't do that without talking to Mom. I just have to figure out how to explain that she wasn't the problem, but I'm not exactly sorry. I needed to be alone. I simply need something else now.

Ryan pokes his head into the room from the attached living room. "What are you doing in bed?"

I lean up on one elbow. "Waiting for you?"

"Shit." He winces. "I meant give me a second, like I'm setting something up, not like I'll be right in."

I flop back onto the mattress. "Can it wait 'till morning?"

He pads into the room and crouches at the side of the bed. "Would Lancival refuse Gwendivere?"

I shoot him a look. "Last one of those for a month.

"Deal!" He bounces up like an excited puppy. "Now, come on."

I let him drag me into the tiny living room of our hotel suite, and my jaw drops. He managed to dim the lights in here. Black-and-gold balloons crowd the stained ceiling. Matching streamers drape from one corner of the room to the next in limp twists. A clearly hand-painted banner declares this "A Night to Remember," the theme of our prom, so many years ago.

Emotions war for my attention. A helpless smile stretches my lips. My ribs threaten to cave in on my lungs, but I don't know whether that's panic or just bone-deep sadness. I look at Ryan as he pulls off his sweatshirt to reveal one of those tacky, faux-tuxedo T-shirts and one of the biggest grins I've ever seen in my life. I love him so much I wouldn't know how to say it in a million lifetimes.

"Well?" he asks.

"You got it all wrong," I say instead. "The colors were silver and gold."

"Dammit." He laughs. "Will you dance with a poor amnesiac anyway?"

I couldn't possibly refuse him. He hits a button on the remote, and the hotel TV begins playing a slow song that wasn't even out when we went to prom.

That, I'll let slide.

He pulls me into his arms and rests his chin on my forehead. We sway in the middle of the room.

"Why did you do this?" I ask.

"This trip has been all about me." He shrugs. "And getting back what I missed. I figured… well, I figured if I pulled my head out of my ass in high school, we could've done this at prom, and it was the one thing you missed that I could give back to you."

Tears fill my eyes, but I blink them away. There's so much neither of us will ever get back.

"What are you going to do next?" I ask.

"The sock hop?" I feel his chin wrinkle with a smile.

I swat him gently. "I mean, we're planning on going back to Ardent. But… are we?"

"Ah." A few beats of silence pass. "I was thinking I might like to. I was happy there." He exhales slowly. "I could probably get my job back at the *Arkly*. You've got a semester left, right?"

"Yeah." I squeeze him a breath closer, as close as I can without hurting him. "But, I don't know. I could finish my nursing degree. Or I could give theater another shot."

Out in the air, the words feel so naked, so stupid. I'll throw out my mostly finished college degree for a pipe dream I had in high school?

Ryan chuckles. "I've been thinking about taking a couple film classes. See if the passion reignites."

I laugh. Why was I worried? Of course, Ryan, of all people, understands. It was our pipe dream, after all. He spins me away from himself awkwardly and winces when he tries to spin me back in. I walk the rest of the way and pillow my head against his chest.

In another life, we're doing this in the ballroom of that stupid hotel. I'm wearing a dress, and he's wearing a suit. Theresa is probably wolf-whistling. We're not going to lose six years to pain and suffering and confusion. And everything is perfect.

"If we could go back right now," I say, "back to prom, knowing what we know, and do it all over again, would you?"

I know what he's going to say. How can he be picturing anything but that perfect night right now? And when he does, I think I might cry.

"Never," Ryan says.

I startle back, falling out of the rhythm of the dance, and look up at him. "What? Why not?"

He smiles down at me, his blue eyes soft. "If I went back, I'd only get to fall in love with you once."

"Sap." Still, I push up and kiss him.

Ryan folds himself around me, and I breathe in his words. He wouldn't go back. We've lost so much, hurt so much, but does that mean those years weren't worth living? I never would've met Heather. I wouldn't have learned the few snippets of real therapy Dana taught me. I couldn't have saved Ryan's life or anyone's. I wouldn't be the Lily I am now, the one about to embark on a journey of figuring out how to just be that.

He's right. I wouldn't go back either. I break the kiss to tell him that.

"Do you think my girlfriend deserves me now?" he asks with a smirk.

I smack him, and everything is exactly as it should be.

ALSO BY B. MOON

B. Moon also writes as Bella Moondragon

The Alpha King's Breeder series:
Bought by the Alpha: The Alpha King's Breeder Book 1
Loved by the Alpha: The Alpha King's Breeder Book 2
Lost by the Alpha: The Alpha King's Breeder Book 3
Luna of the Alpha: The Alpha King's Breeder Book 4
Legacy of the Alpha: The Alpha Kings's Breeder Book 5
Daughter of the Alpha: The Alpha King's Breeder Book 6
Descendants of the Alpha: The Alpha King's Breeder Book 7
Shadow of the Alpha: The Alpha King's Breeder Book 8
Son of the Alpha: The Alpha King's Breeder Book 9
Spare of the Alpha: The Alpha King's Breeder Book 10
The Luna's Vampire Prince series:
The Culling
The Kingdom
The Conquered
Pregnant With Four Alphas' Babies
Chosen As the Breeder
Mated to Four Alphas
Threats Against the Breeder
At War for the Breeder
The Stolen Breeder
Four Alphas, Four Babies
Becoming the Luna Queen
Descendants of the Breeder

Desired by the Devil series

Whispers of the Devil

Banter of the Devil (releases 10/15/2024)

The Mafia Kings series

Indebted to the Mafia King

<u>Loved by the Mafia King</u>

Claimed by the Mafia King (releases 11/15/2024)

Sign up for Bella's newsletter here.

Follow Bella on Facebook here.